Bashful

LO BRYNOLF

A Lo Brynolf

ISBN-13: 978-1986506977
ISBN-10: 1986506975

Cover Design: Alyssa Garcia, *Uplifting Designs*

Editing & Proofreading: Emily A. Lawrence, *Lawrence Editing*

Interior Formatting: Juliana Cabrera, *Jersey Girl Design*

First Edition: March 2018

10 9 8 7 6 5 4 3 2 1

For my three tiny-humans. Never give up on your dreams.

One

IT'S OKAY TO BE SINGLE AT THIS POINT IN MY LIFE. I'M twenty-one. With Evie as my roommate, I don't need a man—she gives me all the emotional support I need. Sure, I can't have sex with my bestie, nor would I want to, but that's what Bob is for. He's good people. If by 'people' I mean my battery-operated boyfriend. He can be a real dick sometimes. Get it?

It's still better than pining away for the guy I fell for two years ago—Sebastian Moore. He gave me a heart-on something fierce. And he's coming back today. Back to Michigan College. Back into my circle.

I closed my laptop, finishing the journal entry for my women's psych class. Taking notice of the red numbers glowing on the microwave, I jumped off the couch and slipped into my boots. *Shit.* My three-hour break between classes had flown by, and if I didn't haul ass, I'd be late.

After double-checking the lock on my apartment, I flew through the convenience store adjacent to campus to pick up an afternoon sugar fix. Without it, I was a basket case. It was common knowledge in my friend circle that if I wasn't hopped up on caffeine or sugar, there was a high probability I'd walk into something and hurt myself.

Taking another sip of the icy slushie, I moved with purpose toward my next class. *Why is everyone looking at me funny?* Sure, it was fifty degrees outside, but in Michigan, that was practically flip-flop weather. Shrugging off their dubious looks, I crossed onto the grass to cut across campus. Catching my reflection in the windows of the science building, I stopped and did a double take.

Before rushing out of the apartment this morning, I hadn't stopped for a second to check my appearance or my choice of shirt. "I'm not weird—my mother had me tested" was written in large block letters over my chest.

Okay, maybe this particular choice of outfit plus the slushie in my hand are a strange combination.

Whatever. I was lucky I woke up in time to shower and put on real pants. I didn't get a lot of sleep last night. It'd be easier to blame the insane amounts of caffeine I'd consumed, or the late-night Internet scrolling, but those were mere distractions from the real reason.

I was about to see Bash for the first time in nearly two years.

The sunlight warmed my bare arms as I glanced back one last time, smoothing the flyaways off my forehead and back into my messy bun. It sucked that this was quite possibly the last nice day of the year. I shaded my eyes with my hand, bummed to see some of the trees lining the sidewalks had yellowing leaves. Michigan College was gorgeous when the trees transformed into bursts of fiery reds and bright oranges, popping against the contrasting green knolls between buildings. I shook the contents of my cup, collecting the rest of the sugary goodness into the straw. Once I'd successfully made the telltale empty-slurping noise, I chucked it in the garbage and moved toward MacArthur.

MacArthur Hall was a two-hundred-year-old monster of a structure that held theatre classes, dance studios, and music rooms. Plus, it was home to my favorite place in the world—the Julian Theater. At least a dozen accomplished entertainers had once graced those halls, and some of their energy remained, inspiring future hopefuls like me.

It was also where I was about to see the guy who'd been giving me panic-induced sweats since I'd heard he was coming back.

Wiping my hands down the front of my distressed jeans, I pulled the double doors open and was met with the cool breeze of air conditioning and the musty smell that only old buildings can provide.

I can't see him. I'll vomit. No guy wants a girl who can't keep down her fluids.

"That's when I *had* to pull out my emergency accessory. I'd rather be caught dead than wear a tie with the same pattern as Professor Jenkins—that crotchety old man can't even handle a proper Windsor knot."

"Hey, Tucker," I sang, rounding the corner. "Playing your version of who-wore-it-better again?"

He nodded in greeting, ending the call and shoving his phone in the pocket of his chinos. He kissed each of my cheeks before opening his arms in a hug, enveloping me in welcome before he pulled back and sighed.

Tucker was one of few people I'd stuck to like glue freshman year. With him, I had an endless supply of laughs and a lifetime cheerleader and friend. I gave him a once-over, and as per usual he was perfectly polished at all times. From his pomade-styled blond hair to his boat shoes sans socks, he was the epitome of preppy-chic. He wore his horn-rimmed glasses with pride, and I'd been sworn to secrecy that they were non-prescription. *"It's all about the look,"* he'd told me once. *"It's like my mating call to attract the kind of men I want."*

"I'm not judging, Callie. I'm simply verbalizing my disappointment in elderly men who can't pull off paisley. Besides, Jenkins wouldn't notice my insults even if I stood two feet in front of him with cue cards." He scoffed, placing a fist on his hip and jutting it out. "He *literally* can't hear or see that far. He needs to retire."

"Aw, but he's so cute hunched over like that. You know I love little old men."

"That's creepy, girlfriend."

"That's not what I meant and you know it," I replied, sticking out my lower lip. "All old people are cute, with their wrinkles and suspenders and anti-slip shoes."

Okay, maybe it is weird.

"Well, discounting your love of the elderly, his tie matching mine is enough reason for him to retire. He can spend all that free time sitting on his porch yelling at kids to get off his lawn."

Out of nowhere, Tuck let out a high-pitched scream. Heads turned as he jumped up and down, clapping his hands together.

"Bash, my lovely fellow, how are you, darling? Get over here before I cry!" Tucker yelled down the hall, hands flailing dramatically.

A spike of nerves creeped from my stomach to my chest.

He's here. Right now.

My body wasn't ready for the instant reaction, anxiety peaking and shooting sparks down my arms and legs. Sebastian 'Bash' Moore had held my heart since I'd met him three years ago when we were both freshman. Inhaling a deep breath to calm my nerves, I lifted a hand to wave as Bash winked at a passing student. Crap, his head was still turned away. Nothing like waving like an idiot at someone who didn't see you.

I stared as he walked in my direction, studying the changes in his face. A once smooth jaw was now covered in delicious, dark stubble, highlighting his plump lips. His hair was longer on top, cropped at the sides. The dark, shiny locks were mussed, like he'd just rolled out of bed. He walked with such confidence—that hadn't changed. He wasn't the boy I knew our first year of college; he was all man now.

Holy mother of hotness.

I suppressed a laugh as he clutched his chest over-dramatically in response to Tucker's outburst. Bash jogged the last few steps, enveloping his best friend in a bear hug. Those two were a pair, all right, inseparable for as long as I'd known them—until Bash was offered an opportunity to study abroad in England for a year. When he left, it wasn't on good terms, and he broke my heart by not saying goodbye.

Tucker hadn't been aware of my crush, but he knew I'd taken the loss just as hard as he did. I encouraged Tuck by creating a countdown until Bash came back, insisting that everything would go back to normal when he returned.

When Bash decided to extend his abroad program for another year, I wanted to die. I wanted to curl up into a ball and wallow in my loss; a loss that was one-sided. I wanted to be dramatic and lay my emotions out for all to see. Instead, I succumbed to Tucker's idea we mourn through fashion. He insisted we wore all black for an entire week. Being a theatre major, it wasn't difficult to oblige.

Now he stood in front of me, and all I could do was stare and act like I'd never seen a hot guy before. *Good job, Callie.*

"Oh, what a sight for sore eyes. Tucker, my man!" Bash spun himself and Tucker around so they were facing the groups of students in the lobby. "What was I thinking being away from this perfect specimen for two years?" he called out loudly, flinging an arm wide as he garnered stares. He chuckled, flicking Tucker's bowtie off-center as he turned to greet me.

"Hey, Calliope, long time no see." He smirked, the deep dimple on his left cheek emphasized even through his stubble as he took a step toward me. His gaze traveled down the length of my small frame, a slight grin at the worn red Chucks on my feet.

"Cheerio, old chap," I said, punching his shoulder. Pulling my hand back, I rocked on the balls of my feet in revulsion as I questioned what in the fresh hell was wrong with me. I was completely horrified. I'd had two years to think of the perfect wow moment for the first time he'd see me again, and I gave him a shitty accent and a messy bun.

Rubbing his arm, Bash laughed. He must've seen the panic in my eyes. "You been working out all this time? I may bruise, Sweets."

"Oh yeah, all that heavy lifting of scripts and props gave me some badass guns. Better watch out, mister, I haven't eaten yet today and I'm feeling a little stabby," I responded, flexing. My arms were toothpicks.

He reached forward and wrapped his hand around my bicep, stroking my skin up and down with his thumb. He moved closer, his worn black jacket brushing against my chest.

"You feel good to me, Callie," he whispered, millimeters away from my ear. The heat of his breath sent a shudder down my spine. He pulled back, his green irises sparkling with mischief. I'm pretty sure my jaw fell to the ground.

Tucker cleared his throat, breaking my trance.

"Hello, still here." He waved largely, almost smacking a passing student. Shoving his left sleeve up, he lifted his arm vertically and tapped the face of his watch. "Yeah, hi, hello. Tick tock, sweethearts."

Bash pulled his phone out and checked the time as well. "Crap, you're right."

"If we're late to Voice & Dialect, Jenkins will force us to speak in Callie's weird attempt at Cockney the entire period."

I rolled my eyes. Tucker's snark wasn't anything new.

Two

AFTER SAYING GOODBYE, I LEFT MACARTHUR and headed toward the Union to meet Evie for food. I didn't dare text her on the way here, because if she knew about my interaction with Bash, her infamous Brit-Brat persona would rear its ugly head. She named her sassy but polite alter ego that since it only surfaced when she was pissed or offended. It was an unrecognizable change in demeanor to most people, except for me.

What people assumed was a cordial statement? Evie was basically telling them to fuck off. With her accent, the insults weren't always obvious. Like a good Southern drawl with a 'bless her heart' dig, Evie's British accent mesmerized people enough that the underlying snark was forgiven or missed entirely.

It was hilarious for me to watch her do it to other people, but I hated when she went Brit-Brat on me. It wasn't her fault—I deserved it. Since freshman year, she'd tolerated almost-daily whining regarding my unrequited love. I'd keep her up late at night, begging her to break down each interaction we'd have, endlessly worried he didn't notice my flirting or how he only looked at me as a friend. I couldn't fault her for being sick of hearing about him.

I reached the top of the steps and politely grinned at the guy who held the door to the Union open for me. My smile faded as he openly checked out my curves and raised his eyebrows suggestively.

"Hey, girl, how you doin'? I've got something you can eat," he yelled as I crossed the threshold of the building.

I halted and rolled my neck, debating if walking away from this jackhole would be satisfactory enough. He probably grabbed his junk while he said it, which made me extra-ragey.

I wanted to ignore him, so I took a few steps before he whistled loudly to get my attention. *Oh, we have a real winner here, ladies.*

"Hey, I opened the door. You going to say thank you?"

I reeled around, my fists clenching.

"Thanks, but I'm not a fan of cocktail weenies," I retorted with a saccharine smile. Yeah, it was a lame comeback, but a wittier response would've left his pea-sized brain confused for hours. Plus, there wasn't any time to put him in his place when my stomach was making angry 'feed me' noises.

Annoyed, I picked up a tray from the pile and stood

in line, thinking about the douchelord at the door. I'd never had a problem attracting guys. I wasn't a supermodel by any means, but I'd gotten compliments here and there on my long blond hair, green eyes, and curves. It wasn't like I didn't accept dates, and I'd amped-up my flirting game in the hopes I'd click with someone like I had with Bash. Unfortunately, my heart found fault in every guy I went out with.

The truth of the matter was, I'd been lovesick for three years over a guy who'd never return my feelings. I'd never be able to find out what his lips tasted like, or how his muscles felt under my hands. It would always be an unrequited lust for an old friend who'd never come to fruition.

Because Bash—you know, the guy I couldn't get over? He was gay.

Three

SWIPING MY MEAL CARD AT THE REGISTER, I searched the room and spotted Evie waving me over from a small table near the window. Precariously balancing my tray with one hand while I held my water bottle in the other, I waved back. Weaving around busy tables, I made it to Evie as I witnessed the Douchelord and his friends chasing after a group of girls. The girls laughed nervously, trying their best to escape their idiotic clutches. I plopped into the empty seat across from her and blew the hair out of my face.

"I swear some men were conceived through anal," I griped. "There's no way being that much of an asshole is natural." Pointing toward the entrance, I quickly filled her in on the idiot at the door. She cracked up, her bubbly laughs contagious enough that I soon joined in.

Glancing around the cafeteria, my brow lifted at the sheer number of men who were staring at her in a daze. It was ridiculously unfair for someone who had guys' attention at every turn to not care about it. Evie was convinced that the only reason guys here found her attractive was because of her British accent.

Yeah, okay.

My best friend was gorgeous, and it had nothing to do with the way she spoke. She was a dance major and had the bullet body to prove it. She had glossy chestnut hair down to her waist, and her large hazel eyes were accentuated by thick, dark lashes. Combine that with flawless olive skin and a megawatt smile and she was the perfect package, all wrapped up in a Union Jack bow.

"They're staring again, Evie."

"Rubbish."

She chewed obliviously as we both glanced out the window at two birds fighting over a food wrapper. I huffed, shoving my hand into my bag of chips. "You're right, they aren't staring at you; they're staring at your knife and fork—because *seriously*, who cuts their French fries? That's how sociopaths turn into serial killers."

She plucked the fry from her fork and threw it at me, only to miss and hit the poor kid behind me.

"I eat like a lady, thank you very much," she murmured, ducking slightly to avoid the fry victim's gaze. "I'm sure sociopaths would use way more ketchup than this, too."

I lost my appetite as she stabbed another fry into the pile of ketchup still left on her plate.

After a few more minutes of listening to her various explanations about what was socially acceptable for sociopaths to do with their food—including a horrible pun about 'cereal killers'—she finally had enough and changed the subject to her next class.

"I cannot believe you encouraged me to take hip hop. I'm a bloody mess in there. I was trained in ballet, for God's sake!" Evie's face was wrought with panic, her voice gaining octaves as she spoke.

"Stop laughing. I'm surrounded by break dancers and twerkers, and I look like I've never danced a day in my life."

"I'm sure you'll get just as, um...krunk as all of the other students." Was that the right slang? "I'll keep your mind off things and walk with you, since I didn't end up dropping Madame Theresa's Improv class."

She grimaced and I knew she wanted to put me in the 'box of shame.'

Here comes the scolding. "What? I couldn't pass up taking it again." I picked at the turkey club on my tray, thinking of the last two times I'd taken the course with Tucker and Bash. Tucker nicknamed us 'the Classholes' since we all admitted our true interest in taking the course a second time was not to be challenged, but for an easy GPA bump.

"Three times now, Callie? I suppose it doesn't have anything to do with a certain bloke who's also a repeat offender?" she asked, sipping her hot tea.

"Bash is not in the class, thank you very much. I just like easy As." It was time to confess and risk the Brit-Brat rearing her ugly head. "I, uh, saw him earlier."

"Please tell me your feelings for him are gone for good this time. At the very least, tell me he grew a beer belly while he was away. Oh, or developed an extreme case of acne. Or halitosis!"

I winced and wished it were true. "Unfortunately, no, to all of the above."

She sighed, placing her utensils down. "Okay, I guess we'll be doing this the hard way then. You need to get over this crush. Let it go and find a hot guy who's interested in touching your boobs!" She cracked her knuckles, preparing to dive further into the topic I absolutely did *not* want to talk about it.

"Don't get me wrong, he's hot as hell—but you've never given anyone else a real chance. You're the whole package—you're smart, funny, *clearly* have excellent taste in best friends, and you're beautiful. But, honey, he's not interested in what's in your pants. He's gay. No amount of female perfection will change that."

I opened my mouth, ready to defend myself, but her finger was on my lips and shushing me before I could get a word out.

"Every girl has had one before, trust me. Asking a straight girl if she's ever had a crush on a gay guy is like someone asking you if you want free tacos. The answer is always 'yes.' Seriously, love, it's time to find someone who'll treat you like a princess and actually *wants* to kiss you."

Ouch. As much as I loved her, that stung. It wasn't as though I could turn it off like a switch. There was an invisible string between Bash and me, and I couldn't cut it. I didn't know how we'd ever be more than friends, but something inside told me to fight for my feelings.

"Tell me how you really feel, Evie, Jesus. I'm trying, okay? I went out with a guy from home this summer. I'm not withering away like an old maid. I'm still in the game." I grabbed my phone for proof. "And look, I joined Tinder!"

She stretched her arms across the table, making grabby-hand gestures for my phone. I handed it over, watching as she swiped left and right. Evie loved to play matchmaker and had sent me on many disastrous blind dates over the years. I was once taken out by her friend's-boyfriend's-friend whose idea of a perfect date was to go junk-picking with him. *Yeah*. She set me up with a dude who drove us around in his piece-of-shit truck looking for metal scraps next to dumpsters.

"Oh, my. Left, left, left, left—seriously, are there any attractive men on this campus?" She brought the screen closer to her face and tilted her head in investigation.

"The good ones are probably all taken or still staring at you."

"Bollocks. You get as many looks as I do. Oh! I found one! Hello, Fucky McFratboy. Jordan, age twenty-one. Nice face, muscular arms, and good hair. Swiping right!"

I snatched the phone out of her hand, but it was too late. She'd already swiped. He was posed in a T-shirt with cutoff sleeves and sunglasses and didn't look half-bad. I scrolled further down and started cracking up at his bio's tagline. It read:

My license says I'm 6'3", but I'm really 6'1".

I don't want you to be disappointed about a lack of two inches.

Sending a quick hello to Jordan, I pocketed my phone and gestured to Evie that we needed to scoot and get to class. Hopefully he'd be a good prospect.

Four

WE WALKED INTO MACARTHUR FIVE MINUTES late, since Evie insisted she show me her horrible break dancing beforehand. After nodding prettily and convincing her she wasn't half bad—she totally was— Evie veered to the left, but not quick enough that she missed the slap I'd aimed for her butt.

Waving goodbye, I added a little pep to my step, knowing this class would once again be a breeze. Madame Theresa was a hippie chick and the most relaxed educator I'd ever met. If you walked through the door and participated, you got an A in the class. The decision to take it a third time was cemented when I realized every other theatre elective had been waitlisted.

The door was closed when I got to the Black Box theatre where the course was being held. It was called the Black Box because that's exactly what it was—the walls, ceiling, and floor were all painted matte black.

Large, dusty spotlights hung carefully from the ceiling, hidden in the shadows by cheap fluorescent lighting used during normal class hours. Those spotlights were only used during small student showcases. I rubbed my hand along the velvet-curtain-lined walls as I climbed the steps to an empty chair.

"Pleased to see you could join us, Miss Miller," a deep, annoyed voice said to my back.

Turning around, I planted my feet.

"Oh, uh, thanks, Professor James, and I'm so pleased to be here." I plastered a Cheshire grin onto my face and plopped into my seat before pulling out a notebook and pen.

When did Professor James start teaching this course? Pulling up the email app on my phone, I scrolled through my schedule and found that Madame Theresa was no longer listed.

Professor James hadn't been a fan of mine since I took his Acting 101 class my freshman year. The class was for basic acting techniques, stuff so simple I'd known it since I began performing at age eight. Since the 100-level theatre courses were prerequisites for more advanced classes, I had no choice but to attend. I'd ended up going—albeit extremely tardy—and zoned out while he spoke. Agitated, he'd call me out in front of everyone, and his hatred for me grew when I passed his challenges with flying colors.

It wasn't that I was a disrespectful asshole. I did my best to focus, but he was one of those professors who was both patronizing and narcissistic, and tuning him out was the best way to cope.

"As I was saying, Melissa, cheat your body to the front. If you face the back, your voice does as well. Are you talking to the wall, or to the audience? Do it again," Professor James commanded.

I watched poor Melissa shuffle her feet forward and start her line again. She was a close friend, but was truly shy to people outside of our circle. Her passion was in costumes, and it was obvious having the spotlight on her was making her uncomfortable.

Her eyes locked with mine and I gave her a reassuring smile. Professor James kept the stick up his ass for the remainder of the class, and although I wanted to sling insults his way, I held my tongue.

"Melissa, wait up," I called as I skirted around the students loitering after class. She was already halfway out the door. "Don't let James get to you. He's an ass. You did great back there. Was that your first time doing improv?"

"Yeah, and I got called out in front of everyone on the first day. Maybe I should just stick with what I'm good at and repair costumes." She shrugged, her half-smile unconvincing.

I locked my arm with hers. "Let's grab a coffee, yeah? Nothing cheers me up more than a giant dose of sugary caffeine after Professor James acts like a dickwad."

"You must drink a lot of coffee then."

We picked up our cups from the counter of the lobby coffee kiosk. Melissa spotted Tucker and Evie at one of the small café tables, and I sighed in relief when Bash was nowhere to be found. I couldn't handle two awkward conversations in such a short timeframe. We pulled chairs from a nearby empty table and joined them, listening as they spoke animatedly about the upcoming auditions for the fall production, a show called Playing with Fire. Blowing on my coffee, I reminded myself to pick up the script later that day. I'd seen the show before and obsessed over it online. It was one of my favorites.

"It's amazeballs," Tucker said, his eyes lighting up. "I'm already thinking of the set designs I can pull off with this material."

Evie nodded, skimming the script in her hands. "Callie, isn't this that Tony award-winning show you're always on about? You'd be perfect for the role of Quinn."

"I should convince Bash to try out for Aiden." Tucker flitted his eyes toward me, and I wanted to smack the devious smile from his face. "Don't you think, Melissa? You're doing costumes for it, yeah?"

"Costume manager for the win," she mused, ignoring his Bash baiting. I loved her a little more in that moment.

"Contemporary options with normal fabrics? Girl, I'd be thrilled if I were you." He smirked, tapping Melissa's arm and motioning to Evie. "I bet it's easier than stitching the leotards and tutus for all of those skinny ballet bitches."

Evie's head snapped in his direction.

"Beg your pardon? My 'skinny' bum can still kick your ass, you knobhead!" she screeched, jumping from her chair and rounding the table.

Tucker stood so quickly his chair was knocked over, but he recovered fast, jumping over it to run from her. I sat there, amazed at the sheer stupidity of my two adult friends playing a game of duck-duck-goose in public. Evie finally tackled Tucker to the floor and straddled him, wriggling her fingers near his neck until she stood up in celebration, holding his bowtie.

"Success! Melissa, would you mind trimming this lovely bowtie into scraps for me?"

He lifted his hands in the air as a white flag and wailed a pathetic fake cry. "Dear God, no. Not the paisley! I'll do anything!"

I glanced at Melissa, who was so unaffected by their antics she'd totally zoned out, still reading the script Tuck had left on the table. I wondered what would happen if a psych major walked in and witnessed this little episode between my people—it wasn't an uncommon occurrence. Maybe we'd all get hauled away to a mental institution.

Evie dangled the undone bowtie and swung it around in her hand like a whip as she considered her revenge.

"Hmm...let's see. We could do full-facc makeup on Facebook live, or maybe he should give that weird lighting-design major a smoochy-smooch..."

Tucker gasped. "Kris? Please, dear God, no. He keeps string cheese in his pocket, Evie. He eats warm *pocket cheese* when he's up on the catwalk. Don't make me do that."

She eyed him suspiciously. "Fine then. Friday night, you're coming with us to Loxley's. You'll dance to a song of my choosing, and it'll be up on the stage. The rest of the time, you'll be our personal anti-creeper bodyguard."

Tucker got up from the ground, brushing his backside for any remaining dirt and dust. He sauntered over to Evie, full duck face masking his emotions, and snatched the bowtie from her hands.

"Done. I'll rock whatever you pick."

I watched her eyes go from jovial to menacing and saw my devious bestie's internal gears ticking away. *She was totally making a worst-songs-to-dance-to list.* I felt giddy at Tucker's potential suffering. He totally asked for this.

Five

"GRAB ME ANOTHER GIN AND TONIC, PLEASE," Evie shouted over the thumping bass at Loxley's. Her attempt to dress casual backfired, the simple white tank, boyfriend jeans, and heels instead making her look like a model as she swayed her hips to the Top 40 music playing overhead.

I glanced down at my own outfit, feeling pretty hot myself. My curves were draped in a cleavage-baring skater dress that showcased my toned legs and small waist. My smoky makeup highlighted the green flecks in my eyes, and the thin coat of gloss on my lips accentuated their fullness. Fanning cool air onto my damp neck, I made my way through the crowd, wishing I would've remembered to bring a hair tie. We'd been there for about an hour, dancing our stresses away.

Ordering a second round at the bar, I spotted Tucker entering from across the room, his arm tucked into Bash's. On instinct, I waved to grab their attention and winced as Bash broke away to high-five the bouncer and Tucker danced his way through writhing bodies toward me. He didn't even acknowledge me. 0 for 2 on waving at Bash.

"Hey, girlfriend!" Tucker greeted, sidling up next to me at the packed bar. "Where's the Mistress of Mayhem?"

Pointing to the middle of the dance floor, we spotted Evie completely smothered by two *Jersey Shore* wannabees. Her eyes were bugged out and she mouthed 'save me' enough times that we got the hint.

"That's my cue." Tucker moved into the crowd to reach her, stopping to pass flirty looks to every hot man in his radius. Still, though, he was our knight in flamboyant, glittery armor.

The recently vacated seat next to mine was filled, and I knew by the signature scent of his cologne it was Bash. His tight, olive-green Henley was shoved to his elbows, showcasing sinewy muscles.

Hot damn, his forearms were gorgeous. Was forearm porn a thing? Because it was getting hot in here.

I shook my head and pinched the skin on the underside of my arm. *Bad Callie.*

Black jeans and his signature boots faded into the dim lighting under the counter. It wasn't fair that guys could make any clothes look like they were tailored for their bodies.

"Hey, Sweets. I'm loving the footwear," he said with his head down, smirking at my Chucks.

I scuffed my soles against the rung on the stool.

Let him know why you're here. Set boundaries.

"Ha, thanks," I replied, sipping my rum and coke. "I didn't get better with heels after you left. I still tend to wobble like a newborn giraffe." I cleared my throat. *Just spit it out.* "Bars are a great place to pick up a guy, maybe get a date—but not at the expense of my ankles. I'd rather be comfy than sexy."

"It's a good thing you don't have to try then." He leaned over and rubbed his hard bicep against my arm. His stupid cologne wafted into my bubble and it was making me weak. "You're sexy as hell, Callie," he studied me slowly, and my body warmed as he trailed his gaze upward. "I'd be on you in a second if—" He stopped himself when his eyes reached my chest.

If what. If WHAT?

Oh. If you were attracted to women.

Removing the straw from my drink, I downed the rest of it without an extra breath. My heartbeat fluttered as I looked back at him, the alcohol burning the back of my throat. His eyes reflected an intensity I was used to from men, but I knew he didn't want to take me home like the rest of them. Still, I couldn't stop staring at him.

Thankfully, the trance was severed when cool liquid trickled down my neck.

"Oh shit, sorry," a voice shouted from behind me, the laughter surrounding his words pissing me off even more.

I leaned forward in my seat, reaching over the bar

to grab a stack of napkins so I could pat the sticky, freezing drink off my dress. I tilted my neck to the side and hopped off the stool, ready to hand this drunk some serious attitude.

"What the hell is your—" My lips clamped shut as I looked up, trying to place the guy in front of me. I knew him from somewhere. "Is your name Jordan?"

He perused me quickly, smiling his answer as he spoke. "Callie from Tinder, right? Dude, I'm so happy to meet you." He grinned. "I'm so sorry about that— one of my brothers must've pushed from behind. Are you all right?"

I nodded, turning toward the bar and reaching over the counter to grab a stack of napkins. Wiping the remaining beer from my dress, I wished Jordan hadn't mentioned Tinder in front of Bash. I glanced over to gauge his reaction, but the focus wasn't on me— his arms were crossed and he was burning holes into Jordan.

"I'm so pumped you sent me a message. I'm sorry I didn't get back to you. Things have been crazy lately, but now that I've seen you, I want to know more. Maybe next week?"

I smiled, studying his boyish face as I recited my number.

"Let me at least buy you a drink tonight to make up for the spill."

Just as I began to accept his offer, Bash shoved his arm between us, handing me a glass. "Got her covered, thanks."

I stood in silence, sipping some of the second drink I'd ordered for Evie as Bash and Jordan had a pissing match. Jordan was the first to break eye contact, grabbing a clean napkin from the stack on the bar and returning his gaze to me. He rubbed a small circle above my collarbone. "You missed a spot." He flirted, his gaze trained on mine before walking away. "I'll text you soon."

Smiling, I backed up to my stool to get out of the way of any more sloshing beers. At some point between the pissing match and now, he'd left the bar. I figured he'd wait for me like he used to, insisting I held on to him in a crowd, because he'd worry I'd get lost. After grabbing Evie's refill, I moved through the crowd until I made it to the small round high-top table where my three friends had settled.

"Bloody hell, Callie! Who was that scrummy bloke?"

"That was mister two inches from Tinder. Can you believe it? Not too shabby, my little swiper." I nudged her and grinned from ear to ear. Evie shrieked and clasped her hands on my shoulders. We jumped up and down, flailing around with excitement.

My matchmaking bestie practically swooned, visibly excited about my potential date. "Did you hear that, Tucker? Our little bird is going to fly the nest," she squealed.

Tucker was lazily swirling his fruity concoction while swaying to the beat. His eyes bounced from Bash to me, back and forth like he was playing ping pong. "Finally." He slapped the table. "The last time she got 'the D' was sophomore year when she failed her science midterm."

I ignored the laughs coming from my two evil friends and watched Bash's reaction. The beautiful dimple was nowhere to be found, and his hand was clamped around his glass so tightly his knuckles turned white. His jaw was ticking so hard and fast I worried he'd grind his teeth to nubs. Maybe he wanted to make a move on Jordan, and he was annoyed I'd cockblocked him.

It'd be impossible to ask him what was going on in that head of his with those two cackling behind me combined with the volume of the music. Settling for a distraction, I stepped behind his seated frame and began massaging the tension out of his traps a little harder than necessary.

"Relax, or I'll make you relax," I joked, leaning in close so he'd hear me over the music, my voice low and menacing as I worked my thumbs into the muscle.

He remained silent, but after a few more minutes, he was pushing his body into my hands while I worked out the knots.

Bash pivoted on the stool and crossed his arms. "Thanks for de-Hulking me. I'm sorry I was being a dick."

"Not a problem. I'm used to dicks."

He covered his face with his large hand, shaking his head in disbelief. I blushed. "Not what I meant."

His smile quickly fell, morphing into something

somber. I didn't like it.

"You weren't careful back there, you know. Why don't we get out of here? We can go somewhere and talk."

No. It wasn't the night for serious talks—it was the night for all of us to loosen up and have fun. He was trying to pull the protective big-brother crap he used when we were freshman, and I didn't need another lecture on giving my number out to guys. I may've been naïve freshman year, sure—that much was evident when I fell for a guy batting for the other team. But I was different now. I'd hooked up, dated, and lived to tell the tale without his help. I wasn't that little girl anymore. I didn't need his lectures.

Lifting onto my toes, I placed my hands on his shoulders and leaned in to his ear. Unfortunately, that meant his damn cologne invaded my senses again. Seriously, was he just wearing pure pheromones tailored just for me?

Take me now, sailor.

Crap, crap—no. We're in a bar.

And he likes boys. He. Likes. Boys.

Shaking out of my stupor, I pulled back quickly and got my mind out of the gutter. "Later, okay? Let's go dance."

I tugged the sleeve of his Henley T-shirt, turning up my lips when he polished off his beer and stood. Stepping into the crowd, I struggled to find an open space, but I was too short to see over anyone's head.

Bash moved next to me, enveloping my waist with one arm as we moved through the writhing bodies.

It's Bash, Callie. Don't get excited.

His wide palm splayed over the side of my waist and his thumb circled my hipbone. My throat went dry. I felt the pressure of his grip ebb and flow, each tender movement sending shockwaves to my core. I swallowed roughly. *Maybe dancing was a bad idea.*

He found a small gap in the throngs of people surrounding us and guided me in, the crowd swallowing us as quickly as it opened. Bash twisted me around, my back against his front, shrinking our space even further. My cheeks reddened and that same flush crept down my neck. I'd never 'dirty danced' with him before.

The bass in the song intensified, my heart beating in time with the pulse of the music. A light sheen of sweat coated my skin and I fanned my face. It was hard to discern if it was from the sheer volume of people around us or simply the man grinding into me. Who was I kidding? It was the latter. Squeezing gently, Bash clutched and gripped the fabric of my dress at my hips, pulling me until I was flat against him. I was dizzy with the intensity of his heat—of his hard planes and my soft curves finally joined in this way. My eyelids fluttered closed and I focused on the music instead of the blazing chemistry blistering my skin.

I don't know how much time had passed, but it felt like I was somewhere else. Nothing mattered to me in that moment—not that Bash was gay, not that I had a date next week with someone new. All I cared about was this second, this simple moment where I *felt* something and I knew he did, too.

The song morphed into a slow jam and I wanted to test the delicious, torturous waters. I couldn't help but grind further into him, shockingly surprised at the amount of rhythm he had. That's when his dick hardened behind me.

I didn't know I could get that sort of reaction out of him. It feels good. Don't question it.

I didn't know how much farther I could push whatever this was, but I didn't want this feeling to stop. Taking a chance, I rolled my head back onto his shoulder, my hooded gaze set on his as I brought my hand up to his face. Grazing his stubble, I trailed my hand lower, scraping his neck ever-so-gently with my nails. He bit his lip as my hand moved to my own chest, entranced with the pattern I was tracing over my décolletage.

Bash's Adam's apple bobbed in his throat and he squeezed his eyes shut. Every nerve ending misfired, our bodies desperately connecting at as many points as possible. His hands released my hips and traveled upward, gently squeezing my body through the thin fabric of my dress. Onlookers would've witnessed the crossing of dancing into dry-humping, and I didn't care.

Thumbs circled the underside of my breasts and I inhaled rapidly—I needed oxygen to make my head stop spinning. I pushed my chest out and pressed into his hands, unashamed desperation for his touch winning the battle going on in my head. *Go higher, Bash, please.* Fireworks burst into my thoughts as Bash's mouth met my neck. *Holy fuck.*

His warm breath pebbled my skin as he dragged them up and down my neck.

"Bash, please," I whispered. *Give me more.*

I wouldn't be able to take it much longer. The throb between my legs had grown from a dull ache to a drastic need. I had two options; turn around and screw Bash in public, or go home and hang out with Bob.

My eyes flew open as my arm was wrenched forward by someone pulling me through the crowd. Whoever it was must've had a death wish, because I was going to kill them.

I shook desire from my brain as Evie yanked me near the DJ booth.

"I think I just got pregnant watching you two," she whisper-shouted.

"I think I did, too." My shoulders sank. *Dammit. Why do I do this to myself?*

She faced me full on and appraised me. "Are you *sure* he's gay, love? Because that was basically indecent exposure."

"As sure as tacos are life." I peeked over my shoulder. My body was still on fire. I absentmindedly rubbed my neck where he'd kissed me, my hands trying to memorize the places on my skin that still had synapses firing.

"Damn. Such a shame," Evie said flippantly,

beckoning the DJ with her finger and a wink. She lifted her hand to his ear, whispering a song choice while pointing to Tucker. The DJ's laugh lines crinkled as he nodded, going to his laptop to transition into whatever music selection she'd asked for.

The volume went low and the spotlight overhead flicked to the stage. Evie's face had morphed into a psychotic twist of delicious torment as she faced our flamboyant knight.

"Ladies and gents, we've got a surprise performance for y'all tonight! Who wants to see some action?"

The crowd went crazy as the DJ hit a button, the spotlight moving to Tucker.

"Tucker Garrison, everyone! Let's give him a hand!"

Screams erupted when the spotlight found Tucker strutting near us, the beam following him as he climbed the steps to the small stage. He stopped in the center and straightened his tie before facing the brick wall behind him.

Tucker was fearless as "I Touch Myself" by Divinyls started overhead. I cracked up at the obnoxious, overtly sexual dance moves he'd improvised—they outshined anything that could be choreographed. Rubbing his nipples through his shirt had driven the crowd crazy and screams echoed through the bar. Bumping hips with Evie, I knew this was exactly what I needed to get out of my own head.

Until I knew, I just *knew* Bash was beside me once more, anger radiating off his body. I tried to look for any tells, but his face was a mask, no emotion to be found. Did I push him too far? Piss him off? Did he think I was making fun of him with my dirty dancing? It took two to tango. He was just as guilty. If he was pissed, then that was bullshit.

I froze, unsure of how to react. He stared at the stage, watching Tuck make a mockery of himself, a fake smile on his face as he whistled and cheered. My instincts wanted to turn and kiss the shit out of him, but a quick glance at his ticking jaw proved it'd be better to just pretend our dance never happened. Being around a pissed off Bash was not bringing up my mood.

I took one last look at Evie, who was matching Tucker move-for-move, and faded slowly into the crowd.

Callie: Got an Uber back to the apartment. Left some water and aspirin on the counter for you. xoxo

Evie: I wish you had said goodbye. You really freaked us out. You sure you're okay?

Callie: Freaked you out? Sorry...just had to get out of there. Too much bass.

Evie: Or too much Bash...

Callie: Yeah, that too. Love you, night.

Throwing my phone onto the bed, I pulled off my

dress, wincing when I smelled his cologne permeating the fabric. There was a battle waging in my head, confusion warring with horniness, guilt, and something *else*. In the farthest corner of my brain there was a perky cheerleader wielding pom-poms screaming 'he totally loves you!'

She's really fucking annoying right now.

I slipped on a tank top and crawled under the soft down comforter. Sinking deeply into my mountain of pillows, I rolled to my side and fitfully fell asleep.

Fingers trailed lazily under my shirt in slow circles, inching upward toward my chest. His thumb brushed my nipple, shooting tingles straight to my core. I watched as he gathered the sheets in his fists, teasing the fabric slowly down my body. Fully exposed to him, Bash peppered kisses on my ribs, nipping at my sensitive skin. His lips danced around my belly button, my arousal heightening as his warm tongue traced my hipbones. Writhing under the pressure of his body against mine, I lifted my hips, desperate to make contact where I needed it the most. He worked my breasts, massaging with his skilled fingers. I gasped for air and closed my eyes as his other hand traveled beneath the hem of my panties. We both stared at his hand working me softly with hooded eyes. I was going to combust if he didn't get inside of me soon.

"Bash, fuck, please...." I groaned, unclenching the sheet below me and reaching for his jeans.

My door slammed open, hitting the wall with a thud. Evie stood in the backlit hallway and assessed me lying there, my own hand in my underwear, before she quickly shut the door.

"Oh my fucking God, Evie! Announce yourself!"

She was SO getting Ex-Lax in her morning smoothie one of these days.

I pulled my pillow over my face and screamed. All I wanted was a little relief, and she killed it in two seconds flat. Mortified, I covered back up as she spoke through the hollow wood.

"Christ, I'm SO sorry, Callie! I heard you talking, and—and—I'm *really* smashed. I'm so sorry. Sorry. I'm going to go to bed now and hope my dreams are as bash-full"—she giggled, hiccupping—"as yours."

six

IT WAS AUDITION DAY AND MY STOMACH WAS rolling as bad as when I was twelve and rode the tilt-a-whirl too many times at the carnival. Outside of classes, my time was spent pouring over the monologues from Playing with Fire. Days escaped me as I stood repeatedly in front of my floor-length mirror, practicing deliberate movements that conveyed as much emotion as my tone did.

My decision to hole up in my apartment had absolutely *nothing* to do with Bash. By nothing, I meant only eighty-five percent. Okay, ninety-five, but I'd never admit that to anyone.

It'd been two weeks since our night at Loxley's, and it'd taken serious evasive maneuvers to dodge him—so many that I could've probably left college to become a ninja. I made it to every class a little bit early or a lotta-bit late, since Tucker and Bash were in or near most of them. Out of sight, out of mind, right? Wrong.

Reminders of him were everywhere I went, and even the safety of my own home didn't stop him from haunting me.

He'd be at auditions. I couldn't avoid him anymore, even if I wanted to.

Huffing out a shaky breath, I left my apartment and made the trek to MacArthur. Time to make it or break it.

Classmates loitered in the hall, holding packets of paper in their shaky hands. Focused, furrowed brows adorned their glazed-over faces as they studied the material. They spoke aloud to no one, to their feet, or to the wall—literally. Theatre majors preparing for an audition probably looked so strange to outsiders. I could only imagine someone walking into this hallway and witnessing a group of adults acting like those zombies who didn't know how to run, grumbling to themselves and not making eye contact. They'd walk right back out, stealthy as fuck, so they wouldn't get bitten with whatever disease we'd been inflicted with.

I signed up with the student assistant before taking a 'cold read' from the stack next to him. It didn't matter how prepared you were with your monologues; cold readings were the impromptu part of auditioning. We were given minutes to memorize scenes from the script that were hand-picked by the director, and if you screwed it up, you had no chance at the role. A tiny blip of preparation was all we got to prove we could play the character and do it convincingly. In truth, we all bullshitted to the best of our ability and hoped we fit the mold the director wanted. To make matters worse, Playing with Fire was being directed by Professor James. If I didn't rock every single part of my audition, I was screwed.

No pressure.

Students filtered in and out through the closed doors of the theatre every few minutes, their faces a myriad of emotions. Some high-fived friends in elation, while others accepted defeat with forlorn glances. I cringed as a guy from my musical theatre class exited the auditorium and slapped himself.

Like, *actually* slapped himself. In the face.

The stage wasn't the only place where actors got dramatic.

I was distracted with the thought until a familiar scent rushed past me. Bash sauntered through the hall without a second glance and scratched his name on the signup sheet, the poor assistant wide-eyed at his abruptness. He turned and gave the slightest nod, so small that it would have been invisible to anyone else. My stomach dropped to my feet, like I was waiting at the top of a rollercoaster right before it went down that first big hill. All of that avoiding did nothing to ease the tension radiating between us.

"Calliope Miller," the student assistant called,

holding the door with one hand and his clipboard in the other. Shoving my monologue book into my backpack, I exhaled deeply and walked into the Julian Theatre.

Climbing the steps to the stage, I gave myself time for my eyes to adjust to the brilliance of the lighting overhead. Lifting a hand to shade my face, I greeted the four Theater Arts professors sitting in the audience in front of me. I cleared my throat and clasped my hands.

"Hi, my name is Calliope Miller and I'm here to audition for the role of Quinn."

"Hello, Miss Miller. We've asked you to complete a two-minute monologue and to read a side from the script. Are you prepared for that?" I could see Professor James' smug sneer even partially blinded by the lights. Whatever, he could eat a dick. The red velvet chair he was sitting in clashed terribly with his mustard yellow sweater. And I was going to rock this audition.

"Yes, I'm looking forward to it. Thank you all for this opportunity," I responded eagerly, polite and confident as I waited for their prompt to begin. Actors had to command a room of hundreds, if not thousands of people, but the *first* audience was right now. I had to win over three people in this auditorium to remain in the competition for the part of Quinn. If I didn't convince them of my versatility, I could be sure Professor James would cross my name off without a second thought.

"You may begin."

Bashful

Anxiety floated off my shoulders and dispersed into the air as I exited the building with a spring in my step. My audition had gone better than I'd expected it to, even garnering an encouraging smile from Professor James himself. I shrugged my backpack higher on my shoulder and headed for the parking lot, excited to fill my belly with a celebratory carb load. I wondered if Bash had gone in yet. I'd never seen him act in a part larger than the chorus in two musicals freshman year. According to Tucker, he was extremely talented but shy when it came to performing in front of large crowds. Something about all the eyes being on him.

Maybe he didn't realize the confidence that oozed out of him, or the natural charm that he possessed, or that people wanted to look at him.

Or that he was as attractive as a freaking magnet.

It was near the end of a long audition day and those directors were probably already casting in their heads. He needed to rock it out if he wanted a chance. Turning my keys in the ignition, I started my car and shot a quick text to Bash, hoping to ease any nerves he had.

Just because it was weird right now didn't mean we weren't friends. Friends needed to support each other.

Callie: Hey, just wanted to tell you to break a leg, buddy. :)

Bash: thanks...buddy.

I'd hoped his response would make me feel a little less uneasy about the state of our friendship, but all it'd done was add to the sinking feeling in my stomach. Fighting the urge to overthink his text, I queued up my after-audition playlist on my phone and pressed play. Nelly's "Country Grammar" blared through my car's sound system as the adrenaline from the stage—and from Bash's text—left my body.

The diner was practically empty, save for the two elderly gentlemen at the counter, coffee and pie in front of them. I spotted my best friend sprawled out in a giant corner booth, sipping a chocolate milkshake covered in whipped cream and sprinkles. It wasn't fair that she could eat things like that and still remain a skinny bitch. All of my calories came with a price. The waitress came by and I placed an order for Boston cream pie and a side of fries.

"Hey there, love. How did it go? Did you win the hearts of the judges?" She tucked the menus back behind the ketchup before pulling out the jelly packets and stacking them into a pyramid.

"*Directors*, dork—and I don't know. You're right about them judging, though. My appearance, the way I move, the way I recite the words. It won't help to worry about it now. It just depends on if my performance fit the vision Professor James has for Quinn."

"Wow. You're being awkwardly mature about this. Have to focus on something besides a certain bloke, yeah?" She slurped her shake and nudged me with her foot.

I flicked her jelly pyramid over and stuck my tongue out.

I folded my arms over the table and face-planted into them, rehashing the bar night with her again. I didn't know how she hadn't stuck the straw through my eye, since this was the third time I'd brought it up since it'd happened. She'd seen it from a different perspective, and I needed more overanalyzing. She indulged me, listening to every minute detail once more because she loved me. Or because I was buying her food.

The waitress came back and set down the pie and fries in front of me, my mouth salivating. Sticking my fork into the pie, I shoved a bite into my mouth as I spoke.

"I pushed too hard. If I do it again, I'm going to lose him as a friend forever this time."

"I don't know what to tell you, love. I've never seen him act like that with another girl. He had you glued to his body, for Christ's sake." She shook her arms in the air, as if what she was saying wasn't emphasized enough already. "His custard slinger was about to bust out of his jeans."

Suddenly the Boston cream pie wasn't appetizing. I pushed it away. I really needed to keep her off the Internet.

"Trust me, I remember. What am I supposed to do? I thought my feelings were out of control freshman year. Now it's...different. Now everything is all wrong. He barely looked at me today."

She pushed her milkshake in my direction with a sympathetic smile. "You finish. You need it more than me."

Seven

I GLANCED OVER AT MY ALARM CLOCK AGAIN, the minutes passing like hours the entire night. The cast list was going to be posted at nine tomorrow and then I'd be able to breathe again. My plan was solid—I'd wait until I had enough time between classes that if I didn't get the part, I could go back to the apartment and ugly cry.

An option that seemed fairly reasonable and not at *all* dramatic.

Fighting against my sheets, I flopped one leg outside of the covers. My usual habit of listing all the Duggar children to fall asleep—my version of counting sheep—had not cured my restlessness.

I forced myself upright and shoved the comforter down past my legs. Padding into the dark hallway, I skimmed the wall with my fingers as a guide to get to the kitchen for a glass of water. Sipping, I glanced over at the counter where my charging phone was lighting up with a notification.

> **Bash:** I know it's late, but I can't sleep. You as nervous as me about tomorrow? You're probably not, that's stupid. You're going to get Quinn.

> **Bash:** Okay, so...good night and break a leg on the list tomorrow.

My heart thudded in my chest as I checked the time on my phone. His text had been sent just a minute ago, which meant Bash was awake, too. This was the way with us—connected yet always apart. Thumbing the screen, I tapped out a response.

> **Callie:** Hey. I'm up.

> **Bash:** I hope I didn't wake you.

> **Callie:** No, no. Same as you, can't sleep. Have any tips that'll help me travel to dream land?

> **Bash:** Nothing that has worked. It's too bad Tuck isn't here. He gives good snuggle.

I smirked at the message, wondering which of those two was the little spoon. Cuddling sounded like the perfect segue into relaxation right now. I'd sneak in for a sleepover with Evie, but she was a kicker at night. I'd always wake up the following morning with marbled purple splotches on my calves, and nobody had time for that.

A ding shook me out of my restless haze.

Bashful

Bash: You know, as friends, I feel the need to be completely honest with you about something.

Oh God. Oh *God*. He was going to finally come out.

In the middle of the night. He was giving me ample time to mourn.

He'd tell me he had a rich, hot boyfriend across the pond, or that he was in love with Tucker. He'd explain that night at Loxley's, informing me he was high on bath salts or something before showing up, and that it was just for shits and giggles. I stared at those three little text dots with bated breath, willing him to say anything else.

Bash: The truth is, I give good snuggle, too. ;)

Bash: I mean this in the least pervy way possible, but would you come over and sleep with me? Could be mutually beneficial.

My labored, panicked breath from his possible confession was replaced by pure anxiety. Bash wanted me to come over—to come over and SLEEP. WITH. HIM. Adrenaline blazed down my arms, my veins feeling like tiny sparklers. It was only a five-minute drive. And as tired as I should be, I was 100 percent awake now.

Did I want to go over to his place? Of course I did. Was it a good idea? Definitely not.

Feeling brave and a little dumb, I responded I'd be over soon and quietly left the apartment. If Evie woke up and found out where I was going, she'd kill me.

I wrapped my fleece zip-up tighter around my waist, my breaths clouding as they hit the night air. Goose bumps pricked my flesh as I climbed the steps to Bash and Tucker's apartment. I'd only been there a handful of times and only when Bash was abroad. Rapping on the cool metal as quietly as I could, I glanced over my shoulder to make sure I wasn't waking the neighbors across the hall. When the heavy door popped open a few inches, a smile and dimple welcomed me in the dim outdoor lighting.

"Hey," he greeted in a scratchy, deep voice. Pulling the door open further, he ushered me inside. "I didn't know if you were really going to come."

"I usually follow through on my threats." I winked, stepping into his living room and shrugging out of my jacket. It smelled like he'd lit a candle recently, the floral scent mixing with sulphur from a match being struck. Removing my shoes, I scanned the room, noting the differences in the décor since Bash had returned. Gone were half of Tucker's sparkly trinkets and bright patterns, now replaced with more masculine décor. The strange combination of glittery tchotchke's and subdued modern accents seemed to work, and was particularly impressive for two college guys. A large microsuede couch lined the wall facing us, adorned with throw pillows.

Huh. I should get some throw pillows.

"It's not a threat if I wanted you here, Callie. I need a cuddle buddy tonight, or I won't get my beauty sleep." He smiled, the snark reaching his tired eyes. "Come on, let's go Netflix and chill."

He caught my horrified expression and laughed. "You think too much." Bash's warm hand gripped mine and I shivered, still cold from the night air. "You're absolutely freezing. Let's get you warmed up, Sweets."

He led me down the hall and into his room. Soft flashes of light bounced from the TV to the walls as I took in his personal space. A corkboard near the window showcased Playbills and ticket stubs from Broadway shows. The credenza above his desk held postcards and framed photos with London landmarks in the background. He looked so happy in those pictures, and a pang of jealousy made my stomach hurt.

What really caught my eye, though, was the large bookcase along the far wall, and I walked to it. It was filled to the brim with autobiographies and history books. I found myself staring at the bottom shelf, packed with a genre I was surprised he'd be into—contemporary romance. Crouching down to inspect further, I rubbed my fingers against the spine of one of my favorites.

"I didn't take you for a romance guy," I whispered, pulling the novel from the shelf and flipping through the pages.

He shuffled nervously, scratching the back of his head. "I've got more secrets than you think." He lowered to his knees next to me. Removing the book from my hands, he put it away carefully and helped me to stand. Pulling back the duvet, Bash gestured to the soft sheets. I climbed in and sank down, enveloped by the pure bliss that only high thread-count cotton could provide.

"Oh my God, is this Heaven? Can I live here forever?" I murmured, turning onto my side and nuzzling further into the pillow.

He rounded the bed with squinted eyes, watching as I sprawled my legs across the width of the bed, taking over the entire bottom of the mattress. Bash tucked himself in, gently nudging my lower half out of the way until he had about one-third of his bed for himself. What could I say? If it were a bed, I'd hog it.

"You can, but only if you pick the perfect TV show. May the odds be in your favor," he said, handing me the remote.

Sitting up on my elbows, I flipped through the guide and finally settled on a show about finding the perfect house. HGTV always made me fall asleep. Thank God for late-night syndication.

Bash lifted his hand, his calloused palm falling gently on my chest. Heat filled my body as he gently laid me flat before pulling me into him. I was surprised at how well my curves fit into his, considering the height difference. The smell of his body wash invaded my senses, which was *not* helping the war in my brain between tiredness and lust. Brushing my chest with his arm, he reached over and took the remote out of my hand. His husky voice spoke softly above me as he retreated.

"Huh, nice choice. I thought you were a perfect girl before, but now I just may have to marry you. House hunting is always legit, especially when they have a budget of eight million and a part-time job of walking cats. Sign me up."

"I'd get a tropical vacation home, and my job would be a professional bubble blower." I yawned, so comfortable now that his arm was settled around my waist. Soft laughter echoed behind me as my eyelids fell and sleep finally came.

Bash wrapped his arms around my waist, gripping me roughly and pulling me toward him. I wiggled my ass back and forth and gripped my hand over his, guiding his fingers under my pajamas where they belonged. They skirted the hem of my panties, barely grazing the sensitive skin underneath. I ground into his hard length, the friction working in unison with the tender movements of his hand as we both worked toward release.

Beep, beep, beep...

I groggily searched for my alarm clock, slapping at the air while cursing it for interrupting another dream of Bash. *Where's the fucking alarm clock?*

Rubbing my eyes into focus, I realized I wasn't in my room.

Oh, shit. That wasn't a dream. There was a hand in my panties and it was attached to a shirtless, hot as fuck, and—I peeked underneath the sheet—well-endowed Bash. Panicked, I jerked out of his arms and jumped out of the bed. When did his shirt come off? Maybe

I wasn't the only one who didn't realize we were both having wet dreams. If he did, maybe I could explain the whole dick rubbing and hand-in-the-pants thing as a Netflix and chill joke, playing off of his comment from last night.

Holy shitballs, look at his dick. No, don't look at his dick. Get a grip, Callie!

"Bash! Um, y-your alarm is going off," I stuttered, creeping toward him and shaking him awake.

Sitting up, he stretched his arms high and moved from side to side, the gesture opening the flap in his boxers. My eyes must have been bugging out of my head—*shit, don't say head*—at the giant morning wood facing me at full mast. He gave me the cutest smirk, obviously happy that I stayed the night, before noticing that my eyes were bouncing back and forth between his cute morning face and something else entirely.

"FUCK," he yelled, rustling the comforter and adjusting himself before turning to face me.

"Oh my God, Callie. I'm so sorry. This normally doesn't happen. I, uh—" He stopped, scrubbing his face with his hands before gesturing lower. "He shouldn't have reacted like this with you. It's not your fault, it's mine. I'm so embarrassed."

Okay, so the Netflix and chill joke is out.

Tears sprung to my eyes as I stared at the carpet, hurt at his reaction. Everything that had happened between us was just fully cemented as an accident.

He shouldn't have reacted like this with me.

Pain blossomed in my heart, any hopes of requited feelings pulled out like a poison. I needed to get out of here and out of his space before he saw me break.

"It's okay, I get it," I sniffled quietly, the pooling of tears threatening to break through the barrier of my eyelashes. *Just laugh it off, Callie.* "I'm going to head out, okay? Thanks for the, uh, sleepover. May you and your boner have a lovely day," I choked out with a garbled laugh, walking as briskly as I could into the hallway without breaking into a run.

Oh my God, I suck, I suck, I suck.

Yanking on my fleece, I unlocked the front door and stepped through as Bash's voice called to me from his room.

Eight

EVIE WAS AWAKE WHEN I GOT HOME, SHOUTING from the kitchen as I closed our front door.

"Where the hell were you, woman? I've been worried sick. It'd be nice to at least get a text if you're going to disappear in the middle of the night," she griped, rounding the island and taking in my red, blotchy face. "I thought you were kidnapped or something."

I couldn't hold back the sniffles.

"Oh God, what's wrong, love?"

I burst into another round of tears, shoving my phone in her hand so she could read the texts and then explaining the bare bones of what had gone down this morning.

"I'm so fucking stupid, Evie. What girl in their right mind would fall for a guy she knows is gay? I'm a freaking sadist. Being friends with him shouldn't be this difficult. I shouldn't have these feelings. It's been years and I just fall right back into the same shitty pattern.

This was only going to end one way," I cried, wiping away my tears with the sleeves of my jacket. "Plus, I've got to be a special kind of stupid to confuse morning wood with attraction."

She snuggled me into her tall frame, rubbing my head. "It'll be all right, Callie. You're going to be okay. You'll find someone who deserves you and loves every part of you, including your vagina."

We stared at each other for a few seconds before my tears turned into howling laughter, a sure sign I was overtired and heartbroken. Evie always knew what to say to make me feel better. She pushed me into the bathroom to get ready for the day, promising a full Bash-bashing session later on. Stealing a glance in the mirror, I cringed at my salt-streaked cheeks and swollen eyes.

Nice, I thought. *My acting career can officially start right now as an extra on* The Walking Dead.

I hopped in the shower and quickly washed my hair, moving my loofah over all the spots Bash touched in an attempt to scrub the memories away.

I left the house an hour later, my appearance slightly improved but nowhere near my normal almost-put-together self. Sulking through my first class, I zoned out until I could pack up again, my binder full of lecture notes as empty as the expression on my face. I desired nothing more than to hole up in my apartment for the rest of the day and watch crappy horror movies— obviously, anything remotely romantic was out of the question. Unfortunately, the cast list took priority over slasher films.

My stomach was having a temper tantrum, so I hurried into the commons to buy a chicken salad wrap before I headed to MacArthur. Chewing as I walked, I contemplated the different reactions that could come from reading the cast list. In about five minutes, that list would become either one of my favorite college memories or the proverbial cherry on top of today's shit sundae.

A small crowd surrounded the second-floor bulletin board, which was common during cast-list day. Hugs and shouts of happiness intermingled in the otherwise quiet hallway. Shaking out my shoulders, I released a fraction of built-up tension and blew out a breath. Forcing my body forward, I took a few steps as I looked nervously at my acquaintances and friends. They stared at me, their faces masked in solemn indifference, not a hint as to my fate. The chicken wrap threatened to make another appearance as everyone parted for me like the Red Sea as I made my way closer to the small piece of paper held up by a single pushpin.

Thudding in my ears drowned out the whispers behind my back. Lifting my index finger, I touched the copy paper that had the text "Playing with Fire" at the top. My glance slowly grazed upward from the bottom, my finger searching for my name until almost the very top. That's when I saw it.

QUINN......................CALLIOPE MILLER

I couldn't blink, couldn't look away from my name—the one simple strip of text that would change my semester. My smile grew as I internally jumped up and down in excitement. I knew it would've been a dick move to jump up and down for real in front of students who didn't get cast. It would've been akin to those prom queens who had an inkling they were going to get crowned who'd then say, "oh, this is so unexpected!" That wasn't me. I understood that every role I won was earned by extensive practice and a whole lot of luck.

I'd been working my craft since the third grade, when I got my first community theatre role in *Annie* as Pepper, and the pure elation that came with seeing my name on a list. With experience came bigger and better parts—I got more and more lead roles, in performances like *The Crucible* to *Into the Woods*. Every year, I did at least three shows and took singing and acting lessons in between. My parents never let me get overconfident and kept me humble.

My back had been against the crowd long enough that they were aware I saw my role—either that, or I was unable to read. Quickly, I chanced one last glimpse to see who was playing my leading man before leaving.

AIDEN......................SEBASTIAN MOORE

What? No.

No, no.

Eyes widening, I checked again to be sure. He was still there, listed right above my name. I wanted to scream at the heavens, to curse them for playing a hand like this. Bash and I were going to be spending a hell of a lot more time together, when all I needed was time apart.

I reminded myself to text Tucker later, to find out if Bash had seen the list yet. I walked backward a few steps before turning to the crowd, my happiness overpowering the worry at how I'd handle my costar situation.

Accepting the hugs and words of encouragement from my fellow drama people, I walked out feeling 90 percent better than I did earlier in the day.

Nine

AFTER COMPLETING MY FINAL CLASS FOR THE day, and since my homework load was minimal this week, I texted my parents to let them know I'd be home for dinner. I drove the forty-five minutes to my parents' house to give them the good news in person. Brenda and Hank had always been incredibly supportive of my choice to pursue acting, my mom convinced that it was fate. She'd gotten her master's degree in Greek Mythology, and when she found out she was pregnant with me, she convinced my dad to name me after the goddess of song, music, and dance. She insisted that the goddess Kalliope herself spoke to her through a dream, and since my dad would do anything to make my mom happy, he went with it. My parents were weird. Regardless, they both loved my gifts, but pounded into my head the importance of getting an education to hone it.

I got off the freeway at their exit and remembered

the conversation we'd had when I told them what I wanted to do with my life.

"No shipping off to New York and secretly working as some lady of the night," my dad said. "I know I'm not in with the cool-kid lingo, but my daughter won't be Pretty-Womanizing her way to make ends meet while trying to get on that stage. You work hard at school, you'll get results. Then you can become a big-city, famous girl."

Mom scrubbed the counters, blowing a piece of hair out of her face as she nodded in agreement. "Jesus, Hank, she's not going to audition during the day and sell herself at night for money. She'll just live in her car while surviving on peanut butter sandwiches. I'm sure she can work as an Uber driver to pay for the bread. Isn't that right, Calliope?" She winked at me. She loved getting a rise out of him.

"She will absolutely not sleep in her car." His voice rose as his face turned a vibrant shade of red. "You'll apply to schools, get your degree, and only then will we talk about helping you out with an apartment in New York."

"The apartment will be the size of a car, if she's lucky," my mom mumbled, laughing under her breath. "Same thing."

Opening the door, it was weird to realize my parents' house didn't feel like "home" anymore. Side effect of being a young adult, I guess. It didn't stop my stomach from rumbling at the smell of Mom's pot roast in the crock pot, filling the air with savory richness.

"I'm here! Mom? Dad?" I called out, slinging my purse on the entry table. Receiving no response, I walked to the kitchen where they usually congregated after my mom got home from work. I picked up a note on the counter, reading my mom's flitty cursive explaining they were out walking the dog and would be back soon. Snatching a can of soda out of the fridge, I made my way to my dad's overstuffed recliner in the living room as my phone vibrated in the back pocket of my jeans.

Unknown: Hey, is this Callie?

Callie: Depends on who's asking...

Unknown: In that case, it's that dude from Riverdale. You mentioned you liked him, right?

Callie: ......

Not a lot of people knew about my obsession with Cole Sprouse. By *not a lot of people*, I didn't count everyone who saw the multiple photos and gifs of him on my social media pages.

Unknown: It's Jordan—we met at the bar a week or two ago? I spilled my beer on you...

Callie: Ah, Tinder Jordan. Hey! How are you? And yes, if you were Jughead, you'd definitely get a response.

Jordan: Yikes. That's quite the nickname. Lol. I was wondering if you were busy this Friday. I'd really love to take you out to dinner. Maybe you can tell me more about this Jughead guy I need to compete with.

I smiled at his charm. As heartbroken as I felt, I knew that branching out with other people would help heal my bruised heart.

Callie: I'd love that. Just so you know, though, no one compares to him.

Jordan: Damn, girl. At least give me a chance. I'll pick you up at seven?

Callie: It's a date.

Smiling, I shot off the address to my apartment and sank further into the fluffy chair as my parents walked in the door. Our dog, Zeus, ran full speed at me and launched into my lap so hard the chair tipped over. I greeted him as his giant furry frame towered over me, assaulting my face and arms with dog licks.

"Zeus! Zeus, you get off your sister right now, boy!" My mom roared and Zeus slunk away as my dad removed his jacket and strolled over, lifting his chair and patting the fabric down before helping me up.

"Nice loyalty, Dad. Save the chair first," I said, wiping the fur off my pants.

He lifted one eyebrow and enveloped me in his arms. "At least I don't call the dog your *brother*," he said, staring at my mom. "That's just not normal, Brenda."

My mom gaped at us like we were the weird ones, as she had all forty pounds of Zeus cradled in her arms like a baby. He licked her face relentlessly.

"Don't worry, boy. Your dad's just jealous because

you like me the most."

Completely weirded out, I looked back and forth between them.

"Seriously, guys. I don't know how I survived childhood."

Mom put the dog down and gestured me over. Wrapping an arm around my shoulders, we headed into the kitchen. I sat at the large oak table, scratching a worn spot in the wood with my fingernail as she lifted the lid off the roast.

"So? What happened? I've been waiting all day to hear from you. Did you get the part?" She blew on the full wooden spoon in her hand before waving it in front of me.

The chunk of pot roast was too tempting to pass up. I held a finger up, savoring the rich flavors as I chewed. My dad walked in the room and pulled plates down from a cabinet before setting them on the counter in front of my mom. I couldn't lie—I missed this. Family dinners were few and far between, even though I was less than an hour away. It was nice to take a break from my version of the real world and just be loved on like a kid again.

I swallowed, clearing my throat as my mom brought the plates to the table, each one piled high with delicious beef and root vegetables.

"I got it! I'm Quinn!"

Cheers and table-pounding erupted around me and Zeus came in with his entire back-half wagging to see what all the noise was about.

"That's amazing, honey! We're so proud of you. We knew you could do it," Dad said, slipping a chunk of meat under the table for the dog.

"Thanks. I'm really excited. The guy playing Aidan—I don't know if you remember him. Sebastian, from freshman year? I think you guys met him once or twice."

"Oh, yes, I think I remember him. He was the cute boy who went around the world, right?" My mother questioned me with a knowing glance as she poured a glass of wine for herself and handed a beer to my dad.

Shoving a forkful into his mouth, my dad mumbled, "That the one who likes other fellas?"

"Uh, yeah, I think so," I replied uncomfortably. My father wasn't homophobic, but he was old-fashioned and certain topics made him uncomfortable. He was accepting, but he was about a decade behind. "Unless you're thinking of Tucker, Dad." I brought the can of soda to my lips and sipped slowly, looking at my mom for some rescue from this weird conversation.

"Maybe that's the one," he retorted. "I can never tell anymore."

"So, uh, Hank, why don't you tell Callie about that new golf course you found?"

Throughout the rest of dinner, I listened to my dad tell story after story about his life post-retirement. I loved my dad, but a girl can only take so many tales of golf and gun ranges before starting to doze off. After texting

Bashful

Evie that I was on my way, I kissed them goodbye and headed home, ready for a chill night at the apartment.

Ten

THE DRIVE HOME WAS STRESS-FREE AND I HAPPILY pulled my keys from the lock and tossed them into the small ceramic bowl on our entry table. The room was dim, save for a few fragrant candles and the pendant light shining from the kitchen. I almost peed myself when Evie popped out of the closet screaming, "HEYOOO!"

"What the SHIT, Evie! You scared the crap out of me!" I shrieked and punched her in the arm. For real, she needed that Ex-Lax in her smoothie. It was going on the grocery list.

She stepped back and rubbed her bicep before opening her arms, showcasing a humongous display of junk food on the counter like a gameshow girl. Evie walked to the freezer and pulled out multiple containers of ice cream, setting each one near the bags of unopened pretzels and chips on the counter.

"I'm going to forgive you for that, because I know you're sad. Now, let's take a look at what's on the docket for tonight." She ripped a piece of paper off the magnetic fridge pad. "First, there's an ice cream binge while we stare mindlessly at whatever's currently airing on Bravo. Then, if you're feeling up to it, we can move to wine or tequila while we rip that bastard apart."

"You mean Bash-tard?" I smirked.

"See? Now you're getting it. I knew I'd rub off on you eventually."

Five pints of cold deliciousness were displayed on the counter, spoons lying prettily at their sides. Only my best friend would go to lengths like these to make me feel better. Grabbing the one filled with toffee chunks, I settled onto the sofa, my back against the armrest. I dug my spoon into the frozen goodness as Evie put away the rejected pints. Flavor of choice in her hand, Evie plopped onto the couch and turned on one of the *Housewives* shows before placing my feet in her lap.

An hour later, we finally moved, stomachs adjusting to the sugar and carb overload we'd just consumed. Honestly, I really did feel a little bit better. Nothing like watching a bunch of rich, catty women argue about stupid shit to put things into perspective.

Evie returned from a pee break, hand on her hip and eyebrow raised as she stared at me sprawled on the couch. "So, are we going to do any Bash-bashing? I looked up a whole new set of curse words online just for this occasion. My personal favorites were 'fucktrumpet' and 'thundercunt,' but I'm sure there are better ones to describe the way he treated you."

I laughed, considering my options. As much as it hurt, I knew that who he loved or not was out of his control. Plus, I was the one who kept putting myself in such crappy positions. If I hadn't spent the night, I would've never seen his dick in the first place. What he said wasn't hurtful because of *him*, it was hurtful because of how I reacted to it. Crushing on him for so long, even though I knew I couldn't have him for myself—that was on me. I needed to cheer the hell up and move on.

"I think I'm going to pass on ripping Bash apart, but I'm down for some good, old-fashioned Internet trolling if you are," I said, bringing up one of our favorite rainy-day games.

She grinned widely and grabbed my laptop from the table, putting it between us. As soon as the computer screen came to life, multiple notifications popped up in the bottom corner. I read each one quickly, the congratulations from my friends about my lead role making me smile. One message popped up and I grabbed the computer, resting it in my lap before Evie could see who'd sent it.

Bash: Check your texts.

I'd turned my phone to silent on the drive back and had forgotten about it while we ate our feelings. As much as I wanted to jump up and fish my phone out of my purse, my full stomach protested just as much as my stubbornness. It could wait until later.

We spent the rest of the evening huddled together on the couch, giggling over celebrity videos and gossiping about rumors on campus. I couldn't wrap my head around why there were never any rumors about Bash. The school wasn't huge, and anyone who was 'someone' had been a victim of the college's rumor mill. Evie and I were once caught for breaking a window in the science building during a tray-sledding incident—hey, drunk sophomores think *all* ideas are good ideas—because someone captured it on their cell phone. That video traveled through campus at lightning speed, and eventually made it to the school's unofficial Twitter account. Luckily Tucker flirted his way in with the guy who ran the feed and got it taken down before administration could see that it was us.

It was possible that people forgot about Bash when he was at Oxford, but the reactions since he got back proved he was still popular here. He commanded attention everywhere he went, and I'd witnessed firsthand how people flocked to him. They stared at him walk around campus and stole whispers behind his back. Girls blatantly walked behind him *just* far enough that they thought they were in the clear to objectify him. He had to know. So why hadn't I ever heard anything about his dates? Why didn't he ever engage or accept the attention from the rest of the student body? I knew some of the vultures at this school, and they were just as bad as the tabloid gossipmongers.

After convincing Evie that she really did help me

feel better, I retrieved my phone and went to my room around midnight, still perturbed by those thoughts.

Crawling into bed, I thumbed the power button on my phone and it lit up. The lock screen was full of unread messages from earlier that night. I snuggled further into my blankets and scrolled through the texts.

Tucker: You're QUINN, bitch! YASS, girl! I knew you'd get it.

Tucker: How do you feel about having Bash as your leading man?

Bash: Congratulations on the lead, Sweets. You deserve it.

Tucker: Are you mad at me? DON'T IGNORE MEEEEEE.

Tucker: I'm going to write you out of my will.

Bash: BTW, I'm sorry again for the other morning. It has a mind of its own, but I'm sorry that we had to wake up that way. I really wanted to make you breakfast.

Bash: Okay, well, you're probably busy.

Tucker: RESPOND TO ME, HOOKER!

Oh my God, Tucker was so needy. It'd only been a few hours since I'd gone radio-silent.

Bash: I hope things aren't weird between us. We're going to be around each other a lot more now. I'm excited to be your Aiden. Good night, Callie.

I responded to Tucker with a quick 'I'm alive' and

placed the phone on my nightstand. I wasn't ready to talk to Bash yet. Yeah, my heart was a little on the fragile side at the moment, but I had to toughen up. The hurt was going to have to be channeled into other things.

Like getting into character.

Or figuring out Bash.

Eleven

THE NIGHT OF THE TABLE READ HAD SNUCK UP on me. I'd read through the script a few times and watched other performances of the show online in preparation. Feeling like I had a good idea of what Professor James expected of my performance, I keyed up an early 2000s angsty playlist on the walk over to MacArthur. I was thankful I put my favorite chunky sweater on before I left, since the afternoon breeze had transformed into a sharp wind that bit at my exposed hands.

Bash came around the corner of a building a hundred yards away and I panicked. I stared at the sidewalk in front of me.

Be invisible.

My self-control was pathetic, and I looked up to make sure he hadn't seen me. Counterproductive idiocy. Since my stupid ass couldn't *not* look at him, he caught my glance and lifted his arm in a half-wave. Was

I allowed to run away? Probably not—thanks, social etiquette.

He jogged over, his lips moving and shouting something I couldn't discern. He looked so warm, a hoodie under his green military jacket and a beanie covering his thick hair. I wanted so badly to wrap my arms under his layers and feel the heat. Gently tugging my headphones out of my ears, he matched my pace.

"Hey, Callie. I know we have to be in there in a minute, but I was really hoping we could talk about what happened the other morning. You never responded to my texts."

I quickened my steps, willing my petite legs to outrun him. I really, really didn't want to think about his morning wood anymore—at all. Not about the length, or the girth, or how much I wanted to wrap my hand around it.

Freaking stop it, Callie.

He remained in step with me, each one of his strides three of my own.

"Seriously, it wasn't a big deal, Bash. I promise. I'd rather not relive that particular moment of our lives. I'm sure it was embarrassing enough for both of us—I mean, you, well, you don't like me like *that* and I get it. We're fine. Everything's good." I ran ahead and opened the door, grandly gesturing with my arm to get in there and effectively shutting the topic down.

He reluctantly stepped forward, his features etched in pain as he wrapped his large hand over my own, the warmth like a glove. I lifted my head proudly, keeping my jaw tight as he stared intently into my eyes. He challenged back, raising a brow, his beautiful dimple standing out with his side smirk.

Don't back down.

"I'll agree to drop this since we're late, but this conversation isn't done. Don't presume to know everything, Sweets."

He was so maddening and damn confusing. All I wanted to do was let go of him, of my attraction and attachment—and I couldn't even force my hand away from his. Bash was the most mind-fucking man I'd ever met, straight *or* gay. This push and pull was so taxing, draining my heart and my head.

I admitted defeat and let go of the door, feeling his eyes on my back. I remained rigid, walking a few feet in front of him the entire walk to the classroom where we'd be meeting the rest of the cast and crew. We separated like magnets, repelling as we moved to opposite ends of the desks formed into a circle in front of us. Tucker greeted Bash with a hug and blew a kiss at me before mouthing '*we'll talk later.*' I hadn't spoken to him much since Boner-gate, too mortified to admit to something. Who knows if he and Bash had talked about it.

Smiling at Melissa a few chairs away, I flicked my finger between us, gesturing between the few empty seats between us. It was nice to have a friend in here who didn't know about all the Bash drama. She scooted closer to sit next to me, binders filled to the brim with papers and Post-its, and a handful of fabric swatches in tow. The door to the room shut and a throat cleared loudly.

"Welcome to the table read of Playing with Fire, everyone. I see quite a few familiar faces"—Professor James glanced at me—"and some new ones. I, Professor James, am the director of this production, and I look forward to seeing the talent we have on and off the stage. I expect a lot from you, and I hope you'll give me your best. This show reflects not just on you, but this college as well. I will challenge you and probably infuriate you, but I strive to make these performances the best they can be. You are all adults, and I'll treat you as such. So"—he clapped his hands together loudly, causing me to slightly jump out of my seat—"let's open to page one."

If there had been crickets in this room, even *they* would have stayed silent after that introduction. Usually a table read would involve some sort of icebreaker for the cast to get to know one another, but apparently that wasn't happening this time. Confused glances enveloped the room as we all hurriedly opened the cover of the scripts in front of us.

[Act I]

[The curtains open to a dimly-lit custodial closet. QUINN and AIDEN stand closely together, a lone light flickering above.]

Following the cue to start, I listened as Bash roughly went through his beginning monologue. It was only a few sentences, but it was painful to say the least. He was struggling, and I had no idea why. I recited Quinn's first line quickly after he finished, hoping he'd hear my emotions and get the hang of the scene.

Quinn and Aiden were characters that had been through hell and back. I knew this show so well now that I truly felt my character was a part of me. I loved this show so hard, because no matter how many times I read or watched it, the various casts brought a different feeling to Aiden and Quinn. Regardless of the portrayal, the words and chemistry of the characters brought them together in the end.

Bash cleared his throat, reciting his next line of the script with a high-pitched voice. It sounded more like he was answering a question during a prostate exam than speaking at a read-through. Feeling his anxiety, I willed every good vibe to leave my body and float across the room to soothe his radiating nerves. On his right, Tucker was watching him intently with wide eyes, nodding slowly in reassurance. Tuck's "tell" was always the readjusting of his tie, and tonight that little thing just wasn't sitting to his liking. He squeezed and rotated the fabric, accentuating the strain we were all feeling as James' glare focused on Bash.

The table read continued, our scenes interspersed with smaller characters. I knew it was a rough read, as it usually was the first time we were all together—but it wasn't horrible enough to warrant the slam of fists on the table from Professor James.

"NO! No, Sebastian," he roared, throwing his

director's script over his head. It met the wall behind him and fell to the floor, a wrinkled pile left in its wake as his eyes bulged out of his head. Face reddening, he focused all of his frustration on his target.

"Aidan is not a meek character! His name *literally* means fire—he is confident and intense, passionate and courageous. Goddammit, did you research this show at all? Did you know what you were auditioning for?"

Bash's face was peaked save for his cheeks, which glowed bright red as he lifted his head to meet our director's scowl. I felt that look in my bones, the intensity in the room thundering around us. I may have been hurt by him, but he was still my friend and I would never leave Bash to hang out to dry. I felt the panic that was etched on his face. I stood quickly, the squeak of my chair legs against the linoleum floor loud enough to turn heads.

"Excuse me, Professor James?" I questioned him, clearing my throat as he turned to face me.

"What is it, Calliope?" he aggravatedly sighed, his face warring between curiosity and anger as he moved his head back and forth between Bash and me.

"I just—I'm sorry, sir, but maybe it would be beneficial if Sebastian and I went through the script alone before we did the table read? Surely you'd appreciate us getting familiar with the characters' chemistry together a bit before we jump in to rehearsals," I retorted, smiling with wide eyes. Hopefully the innocent look I had on my face would placate him enough to give me a couple of days to prep with Bash. Our eyes met, and he softened slightly.

"Very well, then. Cast, you may leave. We will forego the read-through and reschedule the first rehearsal for some time next week. This had better work out well, Miss Miller. I'm holding you accountable. And, Bash, get your act together—soon. Crew, stay behind so you can listen to what I've planned out for this production," he said, waving out the group of us he no longer needed.

Bash stood outside the door, mingling with the rest of the cast before he spotted me exiting the room. It was obvious he'd held back for me. I really hoped it wasn't to talk more about the other night. He excused himself from the group and they dispersed, leaving us alone in the mutedly-lit corridor.

"Thanks for rescuing me back there, Sweets." He strode closer carefully, reluctantly touching my upper arm. "I don't know what happened, and I know I didn't deserve the save, but I owe you."

The contact burned and I willed the feeling away. I stepped back, intently studying the bulletin board pinned with job openings and Craigslist ads a few feet away. I heard him sigh and snuck a glance, sad to witness the internal warring going on in his head. His shirt lifted a few inches as he put his hands on his face, exposing the tight ridges on his stomach. I couldn't help but notice the small tuft of hair below his belly button. I wanted to trace it and see where it ended.

Focus, horndog. He's upset. And you're still upset, too.

"I can't believe I just choked like that. After you told me about Playing with Fire freshman year, I watched it and HAD to do it. I even saw it when I was in England, twice." He shrugged. "Then I busted my ass, put myself out there to get the lead, and freaking blew it. James should just replace me with the understudy," he spouted off in an anxiety-filled tangent.

I gawked as he raked his hands through his hair, pacing from wall to wall.

Panic rose from my chest to my cheeks, the need to help him anchoring me in place. I made a promise in front of the entire cast and crew to help, and I had to follow through. Especially now, when I was crumbling at the thought of him not being my costar. I brought my fist to my mouth and bit down slightly on my thumb, a habit that hadn't escaped my childhood. Pushing forward off the wall, I reached up and rubbed the hard muscles of his back while he stared at the floor.

"It's going to be okay, friend. It wasn't as bad as you think. Professor James is a douche-canoe, you know that. And anyway, his hissy fit was weak. My two-year-old cousin can do *much* better," I said, trying to lighten the mood. "I'll help you—we can work through the script together, okay? We'll get down to the bare bones of it all and get it to where YOU think Aidan should be."

I moved my hand upward, kneading tense muscles until I reached his shoulder.

Why did I freaking massage him all the time? Maybe

I should put gay-crush-masseuse in my *job-prospects-after-failing-as-a-professional-actress* pile. It'd go nicely next to binge-watching-expert and Funyuns-critic.

Covering my hand with his own, he turned to look at me and nodded in agreement. His irises had shifted from their usual vibrant green to almost emerald, the color clouded by anger and sadness. I hated that he was still so down. My stomach grumbled, and words flew out of my mouth before I could question them.

"All right, my dear. No more bumming. It's time for carbs, caffeine, and cramming. We're going to read the crap out of this script, so bring a pencil. Get your big boy pants on, because I'm taking you to the best twenty-four seven hole-in-the-wall you'll ever find."

"You had me at cramming."

Twelve

BASH STARED AT MY BLUE CHEVY AVEO LIKE IT was a puzzle, his head tilting as I gestured to the passenger side. Watching him try to finagle his legs to fit was hilarious, since he'd forgotten to move the seat back before he got in. I laughed the entire ten-minute drive from campus to the restaurant. Our small downtown area was charming, a square mile at most of bars and boutiques. The streets were lined with lampposts every few feet, decorated in leaves and pumpkins for the season. I pulled off the main strip and pulled into a dimly-lit alley parking lot.

"Um, remind me to drive next time we go anywhere," he whined, unclicking his seat belt and getting out. "I think I got a cramp."

"You're fine, Gigantor." I laughed and locked my car before walking around the back end. "So, this is Chet's." I gestured to the dark building, a simple light fixture highlighting the small hand-painted sign over a plain metal door. The glass panes were frosted, concealing the inside.

"You took me to get murdered? Awesome. Did you bring the duct tape and garbage bags, or does Chet provide them for us?" He stuffed his hands into his pockets. His breath clouded the air as I grabbed his arm and dragged him to the door.

"Don't worry, I picked up zip ties and a shovel this morning. We don't need Chet's supplies."

Walking in, the environment was much less ominous than it was outside. Old Tiffany-style lamps hung above each dark-stained table, the red leather booths accentuated by age. It wasn't the prettiest place, but there was no doubt they had the best "study food" around. Evie and I had stumbled upon Chet's last year after the bars had closed, our group of friends desperate for some grease to soak up the alcohol. It probably wasn't the best for a group of drunk girls to be alone in an alley at 2:00 a.m., but thanks to Chet, we got home safely in cabs and none of us were hungover the next day. The food was magic, I swear.

The 'seat yourself' sign was up per usual, not surprising since I'd never seen a hostess here. That was the best part about these little hole-in-the-wall places; you got great service, hot food, and no one bothered you to leave when you were finished.

We ordered a few coffees from Aggie, Chet's wife, before settling in on the task at hand.

Bash and I worked through the script for hours

before we had to stop. I heard his stomach grumble underneath his white T-shirt, which was tight enough I could see the indentation of his abs if I stared hard enough.

Not that I was, or anything—friends don't stare at each other's abs.

I cleared my throat as I handed him a menu.

"You're either hungry or your stomach is doing an incredible impression of a whale's mating call."

He lifted his shirt, smacking the defined planes of his ab muscles.

"Nah, that was just me trying to scare away all of the other stomachs. Putting your hand near my food should come with its own warning label. It's the only time I get scary."

We ordered—a triple cheeseburger and chili fries for him, and a cheddar-bacon ranch burger for me. We needed the sustenance, or at least that's what I told myself. In reality, I was more interested in staring at Bash, but the food here was so good I couldn't say no.

When it arrived, I took a giant bite out of my burger and groaned, closing my eyes. I savored the bite like it was my last meal on death row. "Better than sex," I groaned. I finished chewing and opened my eyes to discover Bash focused on me, still holding his uneaten burger, the juices dripping onto the plate below.

"What, do I have something on my face?" I asked, shaking him from the fog. I wiped around my mouth with the back of my hand but came back empty.

He put his still-untouched burger down and clenched his water glass, chugging until there was nothing left.

"No, I've just never seen any girl that into eating meat before," he coughed. "That was, uh, that was something."

"Glad you enjoyed the show." I laughed. Of course, he liked it whenever someone gorged on *meat*. "Want to try some?" I offered, holding my burger out and he took a huge bite. "I'll taste yours, too, if you'll let me."

His eyebrows shot up mid-chew.

"Come on, let me try your meat."

At the realization of what I'd just implied, my cheeks went pink and I covered my face with my hands. I was going to slide under the table and just disappear. I was tiny enough, maybe he wouldn't notice if I pulled a vanishing act.

"Oh my God, that is NOT what I meant," I mumbled, peeking through my fingers.

Bash was doubled over, pounding his fist on the table to mute his laughter. I folded my arms and gave him my best scowl, waiting for him to finish.

Wiping his tears, his dimple still on full display, he finally had enough breath to speak.

"I missed this. That was everything, Callie. Can we please hang out all the time? I don't know if I can live without you ever again."

I grabbed one of his chili fries, hoping my hand wouldn't be stabbed with a fork from his "no one touches my food" proclamation earlier. If I really wanted to give this friendship a chance, I needed to shove all thoughts of romantic feelings for Bash out the window. The truth was, I wanted him in my life, and if being friends was all I got, I'd take it.

And if I ever met his man-friend, I'd find a way to deal with that jealousy.

"I'm not going anywhere. The past is in the past. You have me, Bash." I smiled and yanked another fry, and he gave me a warning glare.

"That last fry you stole can be in the past, too," he replied, picking up his script again. "Many a friendship has ended over chili fries."

"Wait, is that like your version of girl code? We don't steal each other's guys, you don't steal each other's fries?"

"Now you're getting it."

We finished our food along with the remainder of our lines, but neither of us wanted to leave yet. We talked about the two years we were apart, laughed at stupid jokes, and the stresses of life. We sipped coffee until the sun came up and our mugs were empty. Driving him back to the lot at MacArthur, I realized my sleepy heart was full.

I can do this. I can be friends with Bash.

Thirteen

THE DING OF A NOTIFICATION WOKE ME FROM A restful sleep. Rolling over, I lifted my phone from the nightstand, my eyes squinting at the time. *Noon, nice.* A second ding alerted me that Evie had sent a message a few moments prior.

> Evie: I'll do anything to get out of this physics study group. The girl sitting next to me has a runny nose and keeps wiping it on her sleeve. Tell me you have an emergency.

Gross. I didn't blame her for wanting to escape. No one likes a snotter.

> Callie: Help. I have fallen down the invisible stairs and can't get up. Oh, the fake pain. Help. Emergency.

I padded to the bathroom and started the shower, brushing my teeth before the mirror fogged up with condensation. The water had run cold by the time I'd finished scrubbing, shaving, and moisturizing my body in preparation for my date with Jordan tonight. I wrapped the towel around my body and turned on the blow-dryer as I thought about what to wear.

"Your emergency sucked, by the way," Evie said as she stomped past me and sat on the edge of the tub. She had a huge paper cup of coffee in her hand, and I clicked off the dryer with half-wet hair.

She'd better have brought one for me.

"You know my wit doesn't kick in until after I've had caffeine," I responded hopefully with a smile.

She sighed and nodded in the direction of the kitchen. "It's on the counter. Go cover your lady parts before I drink that one as well."

I scurried to my bedroom, throwing on a thermal and leggings and quickly finger-combing my hair. On my way out, I glanced in the mirror and studied the bags under my eyes. I looked like a hot mess, but staying up all night with Bash had been worth it. Shuffling out to the kitchen, I hopped onto the counter, my legs swinging as I sipped the coffee she'd brought me. Evie was at the sink, rinsing leaves of romaine lettuce.

"So, you didn't come home until early morning," she alluded with a wink, followed by a face of epiphany. "OH MY GOD. You were genital-bonding, weren't you?"

"I'm sorry, we were what?"

"You know, did he..." she implied as she chopped onion. "Park the beef bus in tuna town? Crash the custard truck? Put a bottle rocket in your throttle pocket?"

"Jesus, Evie, what the hell did they teach you in the UK?"

"Did he put ranch in your hidden valley?"

"You did not just insult ranch like that."

"Did he tweet, skeet, and delete?"

"GOOD GOD, WOMAN!"

She reared her head back and howled with laughter as she picked up a carton of cherry tomatoes. "Remember when I looked up all those insults? I may have gone down the rabbit hole."

"Seriously, I'm changing the Wi-Fi password. And no, we didn't bump uglies—that's a *normal* euphemism, just FYI." I hopped down and onto a stool. Disregarding her temporary insanity, I filled her in on the actual events of the night before as she made our lunch.

"Bash had a meltdown during the table read and was super bummed, so I took him to Chet's to go through the script. After like six hours, we'd broken down every line on those pages. We even did some enunciation exercises and ran through some of his longer monologues," I explained.

Evie scrunched her face quizzically.

"You know, like *peter piper picked a peck of pickled peppers*. Anyway, I think he's feeling really great about it now."

Evie grabbed a container of sliced chicken from the fridge and began tossing it with the rest of the ingredients. Her lips upturned.

"He'd be feeling even better if you *puckered his peter*."

Groaning, I rolled my eyes and lifted the bowl of

salad out of her hands, dishing it onto plates. She turned to the refrigerator and came back with an armful of plastic bottles.

"What dressing do you want?"

"Anything but ranch."

After lunch—and twenty minutes of baby animal videos to cleanse my brain of Evie's new vernacular—I changed out of my clothes and turned to the closet in my undies. I needed to try on different options for tonight. Thumbing through my shirts, I heard a knock at the door and nearly jumped out of my skin. The towel from my earlier shower was still on the bed and I yanked it to quickly cover myself.

"Evie! Can you get that, please? I'm kind of really freaking naked right now!" I waited for a return voice, but no response came as another rap on the front door echoed through the apartment. *Where the hell is she?* I rushed into the hallway as the knock rapped for a third time. *Seriously, it better be Publisher's Clearing House with one of those million-dollar checks.*

"I'm coming, God," I shouted before I pulled the door open.

Tucker and Bash stood in the threshold, smiles giant and eyes hopeful as they held drink carriers full of coffee and smoothies.

"Hell yes, bitch! That's what she said!" Tucker

grinned widely, sashaying past me and setting the drinks on the table.

"Oh, like you would know, Tuck." I smacked him. "What are you guys doing here?"

"Well, we were going to see if you wanted to run lines again with this piece of man-meat." Tucker pointed at Bash behind him. "I tried to assist him, but I think he's got performance anxiety."

He nudged me and spoke under his breath. "Hope that's not a problem in every area of his life, if you know what I mean."

Bash approached, flicking Tucker's ear as he passed. "For acting like a little bitch sometimes, he sucks at trying to be a girl. Anyway, I hoped if I bribed you with smoothies, you'd be more amenable. You like strawberry mango, right?"

One eyebrow perked up as I turned my head to the table, the pink smoothies in the holder making my mouth water. They *did* look good. I mean, I wasn't above bribes. Turning, I half-expected Bash to wear a puppy-dog look on his face, begging for more help— but his eyes were focused lower. I rolled my eyes.

Yes, they're boobs. Every girl has them.

Tightening the towel around my boobs, I cleared my throat to snap him out of it.

"Fine, but not for long, okay? I have plans later. Let me just go throw something on."

Just as I finished clasping my navy lace bra shut, my door creaked open. Spinning around, I spotted Bash standing just inside my room, hip resting on my dresser. I quickly grabbed the gray Michigan College hoodie from my desk chair and slipped it on.

"What the hell, Bash! Haven't you heard of knocking? I was freaking naked!" I screeched.

"I thought friends didn't need to knock. Nice bra, by the way," he smarmed. Plucking something from the open drawer next to him, he held the object closer to his face to inspect it. "Try on this one next." He laughed, throwing the bundle of fabric toward me.

I dove forward and caught the black lacy number in my hands.

"I'm going to kill you!" I rushed toward him, shoving the lingerie back into my underwear drawer and slamming it closed. "Keep your hands out of my panties!"

He put his hands up in defeat, laughing the entire time. "Scout's honor," he said, backing away slightly. "So, what are these plans you mentioned?"

"Huh?"

"You brought up that you couldn't help for long because you had plans tonight. What are you doing?" He turned, checking out the mess on my desk as he awaited my answer.

"Oh, that," I responded, picking up a stack of papers to straighten them. *We're friends. Just spit it out, Callie.* "I've got a date tonight."

Without giving him room for a rebuttal, I skirted around him and into the hallway, talking over one shoulder. "Let's run lines, shall we?"

Bash followed closely behind, and I felt a shift of energy in the air. *Weird*. Whatever friendly connection we had last night had changed, and I didn't know why.

Tucker was seated on the couch, flipping through the stack of celebrity gossip magazines we kept on the coffee table. I plopped down next to him, pulling the script from my backpack, and motioned for Bash to do the same. He stood in front of the TV with his arms crossed, staring at me like I was supposed to answer a question he never asked.

"Uh, so...everything okay, guys?" Tucker looked back and forth between us, confusion marring his face.

The vibe between us was electric, and it was possible that if I looked at Bash right now, I'd get shocked. I turned to Tucker, nodding as I opened to the first scene.

Fourteen

"WOMAN! COME HELP ME, PLEASE? I HAVE LIKE ten outfits picked out and nothing to freaking wear," I called out, wishing I had a shot of tequila to calm my nerves about my date. Jordan was supposed to be here *right now*. I still needed to touch up my makeup and do a final hair spritz before I could call myself ready. Early 2000s pop hits played loudly from my docking station, which was the second-best option next to alcohol. I wiggled slightly to the bass—Ja Rule was my jam.

"All right, let's have a dekko," she announced, and I shot her a quizzical glare. "You really need to remember my slang is different than yours. Dekko is look." She took in the piles of cotton-poly blends strewn about my bed. "Did your closet have a seizure?"

"It wasn't a seizure, just a small spasm."

She picked up each item of clothing one by one and dismissed them just as fast, flicking them higher up on the bed into a separate pile of obvious *nos*. Holding up a small bandage dress—trust me, those things look freaking TINY when they aren't on your body—she pursed her lips and tilted her head.

"Put this on, with your gold crushed-velvet heels. Add some smoky shadow—it'll really make your green eyes pop."

I smiled in relief, rushing to the bathroom. Wrestling into the tight fabric, I smoothed it over my hips as the bell rang. *Shit*. He was here on time. I quickly ran gray shadow over my lids and blended furiously with my fingers before scurrying to buckle the straps of my heels.

I overheard the deep rumble of his voice mixed with Evie's as I grabbed my clutch and carefully walked into the living room. *Don't walk like a baby prostitute*, I thought to myself as I tried my best to look sexy and move in my heels at the same time.

Jordan looked hot, I couldn't lie. His dirty blond hair was spiked messily with gel, and his jaw was shaved smooth. Casual but attractive, his black sports coat over a cream sweater went nicely with dark loafers and fitted jeans. He appraised me, his gaze roaming from my polished toes up to the loose blond curls I'd finished styling minutes earlier.

"Wow. You look amazing, Callie. I'm a lucky guy," he said, his Adam's apple bobbing as he spoke.

I blushed hard, feeling the redness creep down my neck.

"Well, have her home before she turns back into Cinderella, yeah? In case you're a hermit, that means midnight, mister," Evie scolded, poking his shoulder.

I opened the closet and pulled my peacoat, rolling my eyes at my protective bestie's words.

Jordan helped me into my coat as I seethed at Evie, my jaw clenched. "Thanks, *Mother*. I'll make sure I won't turn into a pumpkin. Bye!" Grabbing his hand, I yanked him out the door before she could think of anything else to say that would weird him out.

Fifteen

JORDAN UNLATCHED THE PASSENGER DOOR OF his black F-250, holding his hand out to support me as I climbed onto the silver bar to hoist myself into the seat. Trying to maneuver into a giant truck without pulling a Paris Hilton was not an easy task. My body fell into the cab ungracefully, but I still beamed at my lack of panty-flash as he reached over to buckle me in. I fidgeted, adjusting the hem of my dress as I glanced around the cabin. I appreciated the cleanliness, noticing the lack of dust on the dash and recently vacuumed rugs. Jordan either just bought a brand-new ride, or he detailed it often. I swung my legs back and forth as he rounded the front of the truck, giggling a little at the fact that even in heels, I couldn't touch the floor.

Jordan climbed in with ease and I caught a whiff of his cologne—very familiar, but not in a super-pleasant way. Ten bucks said it was from one of those preppy, expensive mall stores. You know, the ones where you can smell the entrance from fifty feet away as surfer music blares inside. He looked like he shopped at that store, so it made sense for him to smell like it.

He observed me as he rested a hand in the space between us. "You look so amazing that I want to say it again." He smirked, his perfect teeth reflecting in the twilight. "Did that count? Because if not, you look amazing...again."

Jordan stuck his keys in the ignition and spoke again, proudly grinning at his cheesy pickup line while focused on the windshield in front of him.

"I'm so happy you agreed to go out with me. I hope you like French food." Shifting the truck into gear, the seat beneath me rumbled as the engine revved to attention. He reversed and left the parking lot, the shrubbery and lit windows blurring by.

I fucking hate French food, and that 'say it again' line just made me want to throw up in my mouth a little.

I reminded myself this was a date and it was the real first impression of me that he was getting outside of Tinder and spilled alcohol. It was time to put on some big-girl panties and maybe actually try.

We drove thirty minutes away to Ann Arbor, a popular town near the college. Pulling his truck to the curb, Jordan stepped out as he tossed his keys at an unsuspecting red-outfitted valet. The poor kid's face matched his jacket as he mumbled something and handed Jordan a small tag.

He stuffed it in his pocket, and with a dismissive

"thanks, bro," he rounded the truck and opened my door.

He offered his hand and I grabbed it, carefully removing myself from the cab of his truck. The building was obviously new, but made to look old, the faux-weathered brick covered in climbing ivy. A large pallet sign was attached above the arched double doors, the name "Catin" wood-burned into it in a rolling script.

"Shall we?" Jordan asked, hooking his arm out for me to take. I grabbed it thankfully since I was wearing such high heels, and we walked into a dimly-lit foyer packed with patrons. He bypassed multiple groups of people sitting and standing around us and headed straight to the hostess stand.

"Hi, Liz," he greeted the young woman, no older than twenty.

She stepped back and focused, lifting an eyebrow as she very obviously judged me. Twirling a chunk of her long black hair, she shifted her dark eyes to Jordan. Pursing her ruby-stained lips, she perked up her chest while she studied the seating chart in front of her.

"Hey there, handsome. Two for tonight? Would you prefer a view of the Huron River or your *usual* booth near the back?"

Red flags. RED. FLAGS. Seemed like this date was his M.O. when he wanted to impress a girl.

Winking at the hostess, he chuckled. "Just the booth, Liz. *Merci*. Don't want my girl getting cold." He smiled and wrapped an arm around my shoulder.

She yanked two leather-bound menus from the cherry-stained stand in front of her, shooting a lateral glance between the still-waiting patrons and him. "Very well. Right this way, sir."

I lifted onto my toes as high as I could, pulling him lower. "Wow! Did you have reservations? That was cool. I hope we didn't piss everyone else off, though," I whisper-shouted as he hugged me tighter with his arm.

"It's not a big deal. I know the owners," he responded as we were escorted to a half-moon booth near the back.

An oil-rubbed bronze chandelier hung delicately above the ivory cloth-covered table. My fingers brushed the fabric and the crisp, starch feeling soothed my nerves. Our hostess put the menus directly in front of us, clearing her throat.

"Your *serveur* will be with you shortly. Enjoy yourselves," Liz said with a terrible French pronunciation of the word, her hand grazing Jordan's sweater as she flounced away.

I looked up, studying the ceiling. *Well, then. That wasn't uncomfortable at all.*

Jordan studied me while I perused the menu, his still unopened on the table. I focused my eyes on the different entrées, not knowing what to say to break the ice. Shouldn't he be the one who talked first? That's got to be some sort of dating etiquette. I was rusty at the dating game, and it was showing. As my face glazed over, I willed my panicked brain to pick out *anything* on the menu that sounded somewhat English, so I could eat here without wanting to puke.

After a few minutes of uncomfortable silence, Jordan reached across the table. His fingers climbed to the top of my menu and slowly dropped it, folding it shut and pulling it back to his side.

"Here comes the *serveur*—why don't you let me order for you?"

"That'd be great, thanks. Nothing is familiar," I explained. I wasn't used to fancy food.

"*Bonjour*, my name is Pierre. May I start you off with a glass of our finest?" he asked in a heavy French accent.

Jordan waved his request off, asking for a bottle of 2003 Chateau Angelus Bordeaux.

"I hope you like red, Callie. This bottle is amazing." He puffed his chest.

Picking at my cuticles under the table, I bit my tongue on the subject. I was a white-wine girl, but I didn't want to offend him.

"You'll love the subtle notes of tobacco and berry. Pierre?"

I watched in horror as Jordan snapped—*literally* snapped his fingers to get our waiter back. *What a dick.*

"Also, have the chef prepare a Brandade de Morue au Gratin for the table. *Merci.*"

Jordan handed the menus to the waiter and turned back with a cocky smile. I sat like a statue, completely uncomfortable at not only the fact he ordered for me but that he was so comfortable doing so in French. This was NOT the funny Tinder guy I'd agreed to date.

"Wow, I'm...impressed. So, you know French?" I smiled at him, my folded hands reaching under my chin in an 'I'm interested' gesture. *Fake it till you make it.*

He tipped his chin at a set of older patrons passing by, flicking his hand as a 'hello.'

"No, not really. I'm not fluent, anyway. I've just picked up a few culinary terms over the years. My parents own Catin." He lowered his voice as he leaned in to me, as if he was sharing confidential information.

My demeanor went from annoyed to pleased very quickly. Not because his parents owned the place, but because the name of the restaurant finally clicked in my brain. Two years of high school French class hadn't stuck, but I definitely remembered all the dirty words. I grinned widely, reaching around his hands for my water glass. My eyes broadened, because this story had to be good. I needed to hear more.

"That must be amazing, being part of such a successful family. How did they think of such a fancy name?" I rubbed my finger along the rim of my glass, stealthily wiping away the remnants of my lip gloss.

"Ah, good story, good story," he said, enjoying the ego inflation. "My parents traveled to France years ago, before they had me. They stayed in a small provincial town for an entire summer to taste a myriad of different foods and wine because it was my dad's dream to one day open a restaurant. My mom stayed behind most days, shopping and socializing—women, huh?" He chuckled.

I smiled, even though internally I wanted to stick my fork through his hand. *Sexist ass.*

"Anyway, every morning, they'd visit this tiny patisserie in the town center. When they finished their croissants and coffee, my dad would leave for whatever winery or farm he'd scheduled for the day while my mom hung around the village. Here's the best part— every morning when they left, the elderly woman who owned the patisserie would wave to my mom and say, 'Au *revoir, catin,*' with a smile. My parents just thought she was the sweetest thing. They loved that moment so much that they chose to honor her when they opened this place. It's an homage to the pet name my mother was given. So, that's Catin. Great, huh?"

I cleared my throat, willing myself not to giggle. "It's SO great, Jordan." *Dear God, hold it together.*

I stood abruptly, pulling away from his side of the table.

"Will you excuse me, please? I need to use the ladies' room."

He stood as well and I turned away, fighting a smile.

"Of course, it's down the aisle and to the left, just past the wall," he offered, gesturing away from us.

I exited the booth, moving along the burgundy carpet as fast as my heels would take me. Fishing my phone from my clutch, I pulled up Google as soon as the bathroom door swung closed.

Search: Catin in French

Translation for Catin – Whore/Prostitute

I started giggling and furiously searched for the appetizer he'd chosen—luckily my search for "bandaid more au gratin" turned up with the correct spelling.

Search: Brandade de Morue au Gratin

Brandade is a puree of salt cod, garlic, and potato emulsified with olive oil, usually prepared days beforehand. Reheated until bubbly, the salted fish mixture is then spread on crostini.

Oh, HELL no.

He wanted me to eat old-ass salted fish? My stomach churned at the mere thought of smelling something that horrible. No fucking way was that nastiness getting near my mouth. I wanted nothing more than to text Evie so I'd have someone to commiserate with, but I was super pissed at her at the moment. She was the one who swiped right on Tinder—she got me into this mess. I turned on the cold tap, inhaling slowly as the icy spray hit my wrists.

Hopefully the reheated Band-Aid fish would be the worst part of the night. Jordan couldn't get worse, right?

I hesitantly walked out of the restroom and headed back to our table, where the slutty hostess was leaning over and showing him something on her phone. Clearing my throat, she jerked backward and almost toppled the tray of a passing waiter. He stood, blushing, before dismissing her and guiding me into the booth. Instead of returning to his side, he sat next to me.

Yeah, dude, you're lucky I'm allowing you to be this close to me after the herpes-hostess was all up on you.

I dragged the glass of wine in front of me, noting the

miniscule amount at the bottom. For such a ritzy place, the prostitute-restaurant didn't appreciate a college girl's drinking capabilities. Quickly gulping it down, I had an instant desire for more when an unpleasant smell wafted around us. Pierre came closer, setting a large black plate on the table. A hefty ramekin of mush was surrounded by small triangular toasted bread pieces. Jordan inhaled excitedly as Pierre left with a short "*bon appétit.*"

"Doesn't it smell amazing? It's one of my favorite things to get here," Jordan exclaimed, dipping his toast point into the vat of nastiness. Pulling out a large dollop, he shoved it into his mouth and chewed. "Don't wait on me. Try a bite. I love a girl who can put food back—in moderation, of course."

Shivering with disgust, I made a valiant effort to keep my face from contorting and barely scraped the surface of the hors d'oeuvres. I held my breath the entire time I ate the small bite, willing it to get past my throat quickly. I pulled his glass of wine away from him and gulped it as well, gesturing to the bottle near the end of the table.

"Too much salt? Did something get stuck in your throat?" he asked, pouring a refill.

"Mhmm, sal-foo-mouth," was all that came out as I forced more wine down my throat to get rid of the taste.

Jordan put his hand on my back, tapping with his palm like I was choking.

"No worries, the next course is way different. You'll love *tetines*. It's a delicacy. Very light and spongy."

LO BRYNOLF

Sixteen

I WAVED FROM THE TOP STEPS AS I WATCHED Jordan drive away. *What a douche.* The Styrofoam box full of leftovers that he insisted I take home was heavy in my left hand as I unlocked the door with the other. Dropping the box on the counter, I collapsed on the couch and flicked the clasps of my heels to unfasten them.

"Honey, I'm home," I called. All I wanted to do was crawl into bed, but first, there was hell to be paid.

Evie padded out of her room, hair in a fishtail braid and a pore strip on her nose. "So soon? It's only nine-thirty. Why are you back already? Didn't want Jordan to put his banana in your fruit salad?"

My eyes narrowed into slits as I scrunched my brow and chucked the shoes near the coat closet. *Nice try, Tinder traitor.*

"Stomach problems." *Yeah, we'll go with that.* "Fortunately, Jordan felt *so* guilty that I wasn't feeling

well that he's going to text me for another date soon."
I leaned back onto my elbows, using my bare toes to
point to the food I brought home. "There's your thanks
for setting me up with him, by the way. He took me to
Catin."

"Oh, fancy! Cheers," she said, bouncing over to the
kitchen. Pulling a knife and fork out—*shocker*—she cut
into the entrée. "So, what was he like? Did he sweep
you off your feet?" Lifting a large bite to her mouth, she
chewed for a lengthy amount of time before swallowing
the lump. "Interesting. What was that?"

"Take another bite first, really let the flavors roll
around on your tongue," I said, encouraging her as
she placed more on her fork and into her mouth. After
another bite, I decided that revenge had been successful
and put her out of her misery. "The date was awful and
Jordan talked about himself the entire time. He also eye-
banged the hostess. OH! The delicious food I brought
home? *Tetines*. That's French for cow udders." I stood as
she gagged, walking back to my room to get out of my
dress and into something comfy. "You're welcome," I
yelled, closing my door.

Maybe I should've given her that Ex-Lax smoothie
I kept talking about for dessert—at least then she'd be
able to get the udders out of her system faster.

I was still laughing as I shimmied out of my bandage
dress and let it pile on the floor. After hanging it back
up, I rummaged through my dresser for an old tank and
sleep shorts. There was something about worn cotton

that always comforted me. It was still early, but I wasn't yearning to do anything but veg for the rest of the night. Grabbing my laptop, I rested my back against the pile of decorative pillows at the head of my bed. The sound of running water broke the silence, and I smiled devilishly. Evie was totally brushing her teeth. Pushing my headphones in, I typed Gilbert and Sullivan into the search engine and jotted down notes for a paper that was due in a few weeks.

An hour or so had passed when a small white box popped up in the left corner of my screen. It was Bash, messaging me on Facebook.

Bash: Facebooking while on your date? Must be hitting it off.

Callie: I'm at home, actually. The date ended early. Turns out that French food and I don't agree.

Bash: Please tell me you puked all over him. Exorcist-style, preferably.

Callie: It might have been more appealing than the entrée I received, but sadly, no. No vomit was involved. I faked a stomachache so he'd take me home. He was a dick.

Bash: Kudos for at least getting some acting practice in. I'm impressed. I'm sorry your date sucked.

Bash: What are your plans for the rest of the night? I'm bored. Tucker abandoned me for some guy named Harold. HAROLD, Callie.

My fingers hovered over the keys, contemplating if I should ask him to come over. Evie had gone out with some of her ballet friends, so it wasn't like I'd be disturbing her. I knew we were friends now, but it seemed desperate to hang out with him two nights in a row—not to mention a little pathetic that I'd be inviting him over after a date. Was there some sort of rulebook for this?

My brain listed so many reasons not to, but my fingers moved of their own accord.

Callie: What kind of friend would I be if I didn't rescue you during such a travesty? I guess we can try that Netflix and chill thing again. My bed isn't as comfy as yours, though.

Bash: Trying to get me in bed again so soon? I told you, I'm not that kind of guy.

Callie: OMG, fine. We'll do it on the couch.

Bash: Giggity. Be there in twenty, Knight in Shining Armor.

Callie: Bring movie choices.

Callie: And chips. And candy.

I closed the lid of my laptop, standing to return it to the charger on my desk. Last-week-Callie would be running around like a freak, tidying up and putting on a cute outfit. New-Callie, though? I was going to wash my face, turn on the TV in the living room and relax until he arrived. If Bash wanted to be friends with me, he was going to accept me in all of my hot-mess glory.

Seventeen

A SOFT RAP AT THE DOOR SIGNALED BASH'S arrival to my place. "It's open," I countered, too comfortable under my pile of blankets to leave the couch. He swung it open, squinting at me while shrugging out of his leather jacket. It was obvious he was assessing my dressed-down appearance—hair piled on top of my head in a not-so-cute version of a messy bun, all my fuzzy broken flyaways sticking out in odd directions. My face was washed free of makeup, and the thin brown frames of my glasses rested on the bridge of my nose. I hated wearing my contacts at night.

"I come bearing gifts, but I don't think you can see them from your blanket fort, Sweets."

Setting his bag on the floor, I watched him right himself as I scooched down further into my fleece haven, only my eyes exposed now. Bash crossed his arms over his chest and tilted his head, focused on me like a zoo animal.

Damn, his biceps look huge from this angle.

Mumbling a response through the fabric, I realized my comments were wasted, as were my hand gestures. Since standing up wasn't going to happen, I just shook my head and furrowed my brows. *There. That would get the point across.*

He unlocked his arms, stretching them over his head. "Okay, then, caterpillar. Better get ready to break out of the cocoon, because I'm coming for you!" Warming his hands together briskly, he took a running start and lunged at me in a full-on Superman pose. I braced myself as he landed, the slight pressure barely felt because of the padding. Bringing his hand close, he tucked a strand of loose hair behind my ear before tugging down the layers of blankets from my face. We were so close now. I could feel his warm, minty breath tickling my skin. He lifted his head higher, his lips a mere few inches from my own, and my body betrayed me with butterflies. Blood rushed to my core, the sudden pulsing making me squirm under him. A one-sided smirk graced his lips, his dimple deepening right as he ripped the covers off me.

The cool air immediately hit my exposed skin, my nipples pebbling through my thin tank top. "Warmth-ruiner! You are such a—a big floppy donkey dick!" I said, wishing my tone matched my *super awesome* insult. I shoved him playfully, laughing when he held his hands up in defeat. His shoulders bounced up and down with mirth as he retrieved his bag and sat down next to me as he unzipped it.

"I have to say, that's one I've never been called before. You've wounded me, Callie." He clutched his shirt above his heart, wincing in pain.

"What, a big floppy donkey dick?" I asked. Surely, he hadn't, considering my weird-ass brain had gone Tourette's a moment ago.

He sat up straight, face grim. "No. A warmth-ruiner."

Wide-eyed, laughter burst out of my mouth and it wasn't long before he was joining in, too. The biggest thing I'd learned so far in this born-again friendship was to never assume what would come out of his mouth. I loved being kept on my toes, gobsmacked by wit—to be surprised and challenged.

Once we calmed our breathing, Bash tossed a bag of gummy bears to me before bringing a small stack of DVDs over to the coffee table. Grabbing the first one, I chucked it onto the floor and watched as it slid a few feet away.

"I hope you aren't attached to material things, because that movie is fucking garbage," I explained, pointing to it.

Horror filled his eyes. "You don't like *The Notebook*? I thought it was ingrained in your DNA as a female to love romance and Ryan Gosling. It's like automatic panty-melting stuff for you," he retorted.

I'd never seen him look so confused and hurt before, like I just told him I enjoyed kicking puppies.

Looking down, I picked at a cuticle while I pretended to read the back of the next DVD. I loved a good girly movie, but watching one with Bash would be too much for me. I liked him, and after my disaster of a date, I knew I needed to just cool it with the hearts and flowers stuff for a while. "Meh. It just doesn't do it for me. I'm not really into the romance scene right now—plus, the book is better."

"I'm floored. You keep surprising me, Callie Miller," he said, flicking my glasses. "Like these glasses—I had no idea you wore them. You look adorable."

Adorable? Adorable is a kitten falling out of a basket. Adorable is a baby giggling. Adorable is *not* what I'm about. "I'm not adorable," I pouted. He lifted his hand, running the pad of his thumb along my jutted lip. I tried my best not to enjoy it, but my insides didn't get the memo. The small flutter in my stomach grew exponentially until he finally pulled his hand away, allowing me to finally exhale.

"Put that lip away. Just let me compliment you. That's what friends do, right?" He reached down and grabbed a movie from the bottom of the pile. "How about this one?"

My lips upturned, a huge smile lighting up my face. "Big Fish? I LOVE that movie! Put it in, put it in right now!" I squealed. I shot up from the couch and heard a "that's what she said" as I pranced to the kitchen, filling a bowl with tortilla chips. Pulling the salsa from the fridge, I asked Bash for his drink request as he crouched in front of the TV console, setting up the movie.

Blinking rapidly, I tried to focus as I woke up. The DVD menu screen was the only light in the room, and I looked over at Bash. His head was tipped to the ceiling and his mouth was opened ever so slightly. The blinking lights from the TV highlighted his features—instead of a hard contrast, they looked softer, pliable.

How come guys always get the long, beautiful lashes?

I must've shifted at some point in the night as I was currently stretched across the length of the couch, my fuzzy-sock-covered feet resting in his lap. Craning over the edge of the couch, I peeked at the clock on the microwave. It was just after midnight.

He looked comfortable, so still and serene. I imagined Bash as a little boy, the same features strewn across his face while dreaming of something happy. I didn't have the heart to wake him or ask him to leave mid-sleep. Plus, friends let friends sleep over.

Cautiously, I removed my feet from his body and covered him up with a blanket from the pile that had fallen to the floor. Leaning in close, I brushed a barely-there kiss to his forehead and pushed a lock of dark hair from his face. I tiptoed back to my room, slipping under the cold sheets. My body was wracked with goose bumps from the frigid cotton, a stark contrast from the warmth I had with Bash on the couch. I willed him to wake up and climb into bed with me, the thought remaining until sleep reclaimed me.

Eighteen

I SMACKED MY ALARM CLOCK, SHUTTING DOWN the demonic beeping I hated so much. I stretched lazily, yawning as I sat up and glanced at the clock. It was weird for me to feel so refreshed at six in the morning. I'm sure the smell of coffee wafting through the air helped, though. Pulling my favorite zip-up hoodie from the closet, I padded out to the kitchen. "Morning, E I stopped, standing rigid as Bash cooked shirtless in my kitchen."

Holy shit. He was shirtless *in my freaking kitchen.* His defined abs were like a damn honing beacon. It was too early in the morning for me to have any self-control. I couldn't look away.

"Good morning, Sweets. Want an omelet? Sorry, I went ahead and raided your fridge—you know me and food," he joked, patting his stomach.

Having trouble speaking, I nodded slowly as I continued to stare. His pecs were perfect—firm, not too bulky, and thankfully, no hair on his nipples. His abs flexed when he flipped the omelet in the pan and I bit my lip to keep myself from touching them. I couldn't stop staring at the small trail of dark hair and that damn irresistible V muscle that disappeared below his sweatpants. Licking my lips, I fought the urge to walk around the counter and stick my hands in his pants just to find out where it led.

"You-your shirt," I stuttered, wiping my forehead. *Is it getting hot in here?*

"Yeah, I spilled coffee on it. Can you do me a favor? I think I might have gotten burned right here," he said, pointing to his lower left side. "Can you check it for me?"

Already checking, dude.

I flushed—there was no way he could miss it. I scurried over and placed my hands on his stomach, keeping my gaze focused anywhere but his face. His skin was hard and warm underneath my small fingers. I wanted to explore further; the struggle was real. I mentally slapped myself, pulling my hands away like they'd been zapped by an electric shock.

"Uh, no, I don't see anything. You're good." I smiled, turning quickly to grab a coffee cup from the top cabinet. Jumping onto the counter, I landed on my knees as I reached to the top shelf for my "fun mugs."

"What the hell are you doing, woman?" Bash asked from behind me, laughing his ass off.

Furrowing my brow, I snatched one and turned my

head. "I'm five foot one, buddy. How the hell else was I going to get a cup down?"

Bash took one small step in my galley kitchen, lifting me off the counter and setting me down on my toes. "You could just, I don't know, ask for help," he answered, our eyes locked.

"You'd better not be burning my omelet, mister. I'm hungry," I said, squeezing around him to fill my mug with morning deliciousness.

"Right," he said, hurrying back to the stove.

Once Bash finished plating both omelets, he ushered me to a barstool and sat to my left. I cut a large bite, my stomach growling at the smell of onion and melted cheese. Bash looked at me for approval as I lifted the forkful to my lips, my tongue running along the seam in anticipation.

"Oh my Goddddd," I moaned loudly. My head rolled backward, eyes closed at the pure deliciousness I was tasting. "Where did you learn to cook like this?" If it was possible to have an actual orgasm from food, I'd be climaxing right now.

"My dad. He's been perfecting his recipes since I was a kid, and I always loved to watch. My other dad would always go home during his lunch just so he'd get his favorite panini. He said they were more addictive than crack. I think he still has one every day for lunch."

"Wait, your dad and your...dad?" I wiped my mouth with a napkin.

He nodded, never breaking eye contact. It was

obvious he was worried about my reaction, his body rigid as he waited for me to make the next move.

I was shocked, sure, but it wasn't because he was raised by two dads. I thought back to freshman year and realized he'd never really brought up his family. It was obvious he very rarely shared this information, and it meant a lot that he was trusting me with a piece of his heart. I smiled, gained my bearings quickly, and went to cut another bite of my omelet. "Well, props to your dad. This is freaking amazing. I'll take that panini next time, chef."

Bash's shoulders relaxed immediately, a huge grin spreading on his face. I licked my lower lip, wishing I could do the same with the deep dimple on his cheek. "I'll do that, Callie. Just warning you, though, once you have panini-crack, you'll never go back."

Pretty sure he was one hundred percent right about that.

Nineteen

AFTER OUR FIRST REHEARSAL, IT WAS CLEAR Bash still needed some one-on-one time to really get his confidence going. I'd offered to meet him after dinner this week at MacArthur to work on a couple of the more difficult scenes, and he'd taken me up on it.

I walked into the Black Box and turned on the lights. Bash would be here in ten minutes, and I was glad I got here early enough to compose myself beforehand. After our little sleepover, I'd made a point to distance myself from him a little bit. It was way too easy to be his friend, and I felt myself getting too comfortable. I couldn't set myself up to fall again.

When Bash walked in, we got right to work and went over the first scene. It was obvious he'd been working hard at memorizing the lines, but he was stiff and robotic in his delivery. He groaned in frustration.

"I just don't get it. I've watched like twenty performances of this on YouTube, and for whatever reason, I can't emulate the other Aidens."

Ah, so there it was. He was too busy trying to be what he thought the character was supposed to be. The great part about this show was that Aiden and Quinn could be taken in so many different directions.

"Stop worrying about every other Aiden you saw. You need to figure out *your* version of Aiden. Who is he?"

"That's just it. I don't know. How the hell am I supposed to get that deep? What kind of actor am I if I can't even act?" Bash ran his fingers through his hair, his face downtrodden.

"It's not just about hair and makeup and getting all dressed up. It's about taking all of that off and exposing yourself to your audience. Let go of the façade. Acting is stripping all of that away and feeling the depth of the character. Can you try that?"

I noticed the sheen of sweet on his skin from the heat of the overhead lights. He lifted his eyes slowly from the script in his hand and locked eyes with mine. We were at least ten feet away, but I felt a sizzle in the air between us.

"I think I can handle stripping down."

Holy shit. The sharp intake of air lodged itself in my throat. My breath hitched and I turned my reddened face away, gasping air in between coughs.

Bash charged over, patting my hunched over body. "Are you okay? What happened?"

"Nothing," I sputtered, holding my hand up to let

him know I wasn't dying. "Just choking on air. N-normal th-thing for me."

I stood slowly, catching my breath. He was so close again, the warmth of his hand on my back radiating through my shirt. Bash continued rubbing my back from the nape of my neck down to the edge of my yoga pants, and my breathing slowed.

I stepped away, cheeks flushed, and gathered my things. Turning to him, I gave a small embarrassed smile and speed-walked to the door. My embarrassment was overpowering and it wasn't only because of my inability to breathe. If working privately with Bash was going to be a thing, then I needed to have my wits about me. No more touching, if I could help it.

"Just...just work on that scene and we'll pick things back up in a few days. It's late, and I need water."

I heard a faint "see you later," before I darted down the hall. As I rounded the corner, my body slammed directly into something hard and I recoiled. Professor James backed up ever so slightly, his hands remaining on my shoulders.

"Miss Miller, what are you doing here so late?"

Was he swaying? Maybe his hands were on me to steady himself, not the other way around.

"I just finished rehearsing with Sebastian, Professor."

"I appreciate that. It seems as though my choice of lead may have been a mistake. And please, call me Mark. No need for such formalities outside of office hours." He was staring at my lips, his eyes unfocused and bloodshot.

Fight or flight, Callie. Fight or flight.

He reached for a strand of my errant hair and tucked it behind my ear. "You know, if you ever need extra rehearsing yourself, I'd love to help. Your mental game is there, but I think you could work on your *physical* acting a bit more," he said as his gaze roamed my body.

My skin started to crawl at his insinuation. He leaned in, dangerously close to my face.

"Some stretching and extra improv could really help with your stage work. I'm sure we could work something out," he whispered, his lips grazing my ear.

This isn't happening. I didn't know what to do, how to react in a way that wouldn't anger him, so I playfully pushed him off with a laugh. I could smell cheap vodka on his breath.

He ran his index finger down the exposed skin near my collarbone, leaving a trail of disgust behind it. He was moving forward, caging me in, and my nerves burned with adrenaline. I wanted to be gone, be invisible, be able to be beamed up like Scotty right now.

I skirted around him, quickly heading for the exit as I cleared my throat. My face was hot, tingling with shame and disgust. "Thank you for the offer, Prof—er, *Mark*. I will keep that in mind. Have a good night, sir."

I didn't stop running until I was far enough away from the building that he wouldn't be able to see me if he decided to follow. It was too public, the street lights illuminating the students who took night classes on their way around campus. Sitting on the nearest empty bench, I shakily pulled out my phone to call Evie. When it went to voicemail, I hung up and texted the only person I knew would get here quickly.

I was shaking, and I wasn't sure if it was because of the cold night air or the shock of what had just happened. My knees wouldn't stop bouncing, and the chattering of my teeth echoed around me. I stood, my body rigid as a dark figure approached from the shadows of the trees. I balled my fists into my sleeves, biting my lip in fear.

Bash's face appeared under the light of the lamppost a few yards away, and my shoulders sagged in relief. He strode over, taking in my ashen appearance. His large hands cupped my face, worry written on his features. "Tell me what happened. Why are you out here all alone?"

Tears welled in my eyes as I shook my head, the words not yet ready to leave my lips. The only words I texted to him were *I need you, please* and my location. He told me he'd be there in ten and made it to me in less than five.

I broke away from his touch and buried myself into his chest. Salty tears fell freely onto his sweatshirt as he encased me in his arms, hushing me until I calmed.

"He—he came on to me," I choked out as I pulled

away. I sniffled and stared at the ground, fearful of Bash's reaction.

He tilted my chin upward, so my gaze met his. His green irises had turned the color of the pine trees around us, dark and stormy. "Who came on to you?"

I wanted to tell him. I just didn't know how. I didn't know if I was ready. The ramifications of someone else knowing—especially on this campus—could take my 'allegation' to a level higher than I was prepared to take it.

"I just—I just needed you, Bash. I'm okay, I promise," I sniffled. "I can't talk about it right now. I just want to go home, but I couldn't walk to my car alone. Not tonight."

His lips tensed in a hard line, his eyes searching for answers in my own. I knew he wanted to argue, to get to the bottom of this for me. But Bash wasn't my boyfriend, I couldn't ask him to help me solve my problems. I had to take care of them myself.

Bash gave me a firm nod before he broke eye contact and picked up my bag from the bench. "We don't have to talk about it right now, but we will, Sweets. And for the record, I will *always* come when you need me. And I will do whatever I have to do to keep that terrified look from *ever* gracing your face again. Come on," he said, reaching for my hand.

Twenty

BY THE TIME I ARRIVED BACK AT THE APARTMENT, the shaking had mostly stopped. I felt completely drained. I sat in my car for a while, the volume on low and the heat blasting in my face as I went through the events of tonight for the millionth time.

Had I given off signs to Professor James that I was into him? Had I spoken to him in any way that he could've considered flirting? Had I dressed too provocatively? Did I wear too much makeup?

No.

I wasn't going to victim-shame myself. That was bullshit.

I did *nothing* wrong—and even if I did, that didn't mean he had a right to touch me. That didn't mean he could take advantage of his position as a college professor.

Oh God—has he done this before?

My mind was reeling now at the thought of other

girls who could be suffering in silence at this very moment. I clenched my teeth, my shaking transforming from fear to anger.

I ripped the keys from the ignition and stomped out of the car. Once I heard the double-beep of the doors locking, I climbed the steps to my apartment and barreled into it.

"Heya, love! How was your practice time with Bash?" Evie yelled from her room.

I dropped my bag on the coffee table and tossed my jacket into the closet, not bothering with a hanger. I moved with purpose. Standing in the entrance of her room, I waited in silence until she noticed me.

"Couch time. Now," I said and turned away.

She followed quickly, knowing all too well that couch time meant we were about to have a serious conversation. It was our trump card. Nothing held higher priority in our friendship than those two words.

She moved slowly, grabbing a bag of popcorn from our small pantry and shoving it in the microwave. Grabbing a bottle of pinot grigio and two glasses, she quickly made her way to the couch. She unscrewed the cap from the bottle—the best kind of wine—and poured us both a hefty serving. Her face was scrunched, eyes squinting in anger. "What did he do?"

I shook my head furiously, folding my legs under myself and facing her. Taking a deep breath, I looked down at the couch and picked at the fibers. "It wasn't Bash."

I filled her in, and her face grew redder with each word. By the time I'd finished recalling the events, she was already on glass number three.

"I can't believe what a creep he is! Did anyone see? Isn't he married?" she shrieked, stomping to the couch with a second bag of popcorn in one hand and a full glass of wine in the other, sloshing it on the rug.

"No, no one saw. I shouldn't have been there so late. I should've had Bash walk me out." I picked at my fuzzy socks, pulling pill after pill from the fabric and dropping it into a pile on the coffee table. Evie grabbed my hands and placed them in hers.

"It is *so* not your fault that your bloody teacher came on to you. Don't you dare question yourself with what you *should* have done. He shouldn't have. He shouldn't have even spoken to you. He is revolting and you need to just stay as far away from him as you can. I swear the next time I see him in the hall, I'll accidentally 'trip' so my foot can land right in his tiny junk."

"I just don't get it. How am I supposed to face him? Do I just pretend like it didn't happen?" I swallowed a gulp from my glass, the slow burn of the pinot traveling quickly down my throat. "Do we have anything stronger than this? I don't think it's a wine kind of night."

Searching for something with a higher alcohol content, I began the lengthy process of opening each of our cabinets. Wasted-Evie had the tendency to hide liquor bottles when she was drunk, resulting in a rousing game of hide-and-seek for me. I spotted a fifth of rum hidden behind our pots and pans—*of course, because where else would it be*? That would do. Pulling a glass from above the microwave, I poured a shot of Captain and reached into the fridge for a Coke.

"I'm just glad Bash came and got you. He's a good friend to have around. I mean—all those muscles—he's not a bad guy to come to your defense. I'd pay to watch him use them." She was tipsy, I could see it in her eyes. It was getting late, and as much as I felt better after getting everything off my chest, I knew nothing was going to change tonight. Lifting the glass to my lips, I took the shot of rum in one gulp and decided not to bother with opening the can of soda. The burn was enough.

Evie's arms stretched high into the air as she yawned. It wasn't just her—my energy level had been demolished from the emotional overload. It was time for bed.

"I know how long you've wanted this part, Callie. It's your dream. I'm not defending him in the least, because he's a creepy asshole. But he's also your director. Tread carefully until we can come up with a fail-proof plan to report him."

Twenty-One

THE NEXT FEW REHEARSALS WENT SMOOTHLY, especially since I shoved the night at the Black Box to the back of my brain.

I hadn't made eye contact with Professor James since the incident. If he remembered what he did, then he was doing an excellent job of hiding his guilt. I glanced peeks at him while he directed others, watched as he carried himself the way he usually did, as pompous and demanding as before. I took his direction as professionally as I could, happy that I was surrounded by a cast and crew that made me feel safe. If I thought of a question or a note, I'd wait for a break and sneak into the audience to speak with the student director instead of getting anywhere near James. If he didn't know the answer, I'd run away before he called our director over.

Improv class was another story, though. Avoiding him in a smaller space was proving to be difficult, but not impossible. My chest would heave with panic when I felt his focus on me during our class exercises, and I had a sickening desire to hurl myself out of the room so I could go home and rub my skin raw. I focused on the clock day after day, packing up and hauling ass out of the room before anyone else had even stood up at dismissal. I wasn't going to get trapped alone with him again.

No one in the department had realized I was on edge, with the exception of Bash. Even Tucker was clueless. I was thankful for that—at least my acting was convincing. Bash had been practically glued to my side since that night. He was always prepared for my quick scurry out of rehearsals, walking me to my car in the north lot before heading home himself. As often as he could, he'd be outside of my classrooms during the day, standing in a visible spot outside the door so I could see that he was there, waiting. My mind eased when he was near, my own personal bodyguard and safety net. I tried to thank him with food and rides home, but he always refused.

"We've been over this, Callie. I'm not leaving you alone until that fear leaves your eyes. I'm not going anywhere," he'd say. He'd walk away without another word, but not before he was fully satisfied that I was okay, that I was safe and sound.

He'd text me every single night, making sure I arrived home safely and that my door was locked and deadbolted. Sometimes after I assured him—and checking the locks again—we'd segue into conversation for hours, both of us seeming to need that extra connection. Those were the nights Bash helped me escape myself—he'd pull the trouble from my thoughts, leaving a comfortable bubble of satiated happiness in its wake. Those were the nights where we solidified our friendship, our connection more intense than anything I'd ever felt. Those were the nights I fell a little bit in love with him, even though I knew it was wrong.

We picked up our private rehearsals the following week at the Black Box. Bash continued to struggle on stage, his frustration palpable. Frustration and at times anger radiated off him in waves, affecting everyone around him. I did my best to prompt him, mentally and physically pushing Quinn into his head, but he wasn't focused. He wasn't *there* as Aiden, or as Bash—they were both off in some other dimension. All we got was the shell. Everyone felt the pressure for him to succeed, because without it, the show would fail. I couldn't carry the lead on my own. He felt it. It sucked him dry.

So off we went, four times a week, to the Black Box. Most of the time he'd have breakthroughs, getting out of his own head and breaking down the character of Aiden. Some days, he looked like he could throw the chair in front of us against the cinderblock wall hard enough to leave a dent. Those were the days where my patience really *was* a virtue, mustering up every drop of it to help him move past his block. We'd break for water, and I'd force him into a chair and rub him out—his shoulders, I mean—and he'd instantly calm. I internalized the immense joy I got from having the power to relax him, because right now he needed me to play the role of the best friend.

Let me tell you, doing that was a lot harder than pretending to be Quinn for the show.

October came and went, and finally Bash's progress was where he wanted it to be. All of the work we put in had paid off, and our characters were more connected than ever. We fed off of each other's energy, the rest of the cast in awe as we performed our scenes.

The only thing we hadn't practiced was the kiss. It was the fade to black scene at the end, where Quinn and Aiden reconciled. It was *literally* the show-stopper as far as Playing with Fire was concerned—not just because it was the closing scene, but because not a dry eye was left in the house by the time the lights when down. Bash and I would be face-to-face, centimeters away from our lips closing that final gap, our adrenaline surging. And every freaking time, it was interrupted with a "Cut!" from James.

We'd pull apart, the intensity of the scene still unshaken from our brains. I'd stand there, front and center, pulling my heart back into my body as Professor James berated us and shouted that we weren't convincing enough yet. That we weren't emotionally involved enough. He didn't want to see that final moment until he *felt* what our characters were feeling.

Yeah, I'm sure that was the reason.

Twenty-Two

"WE'VE GOT FOUR COSTUME CHANGES FOR THE show and about fifty options," Melissa said.

I slapped my forehead and huffed out a breath, overwhelmed at all the textures and colors of the fabrics.

"Jeez, Callie. Don't get so excited," she muttered, with a roll of her eyes. "Come on, girl, get down to your skivvies. We've only got an hour before the guys show up."

I loved costumes when they were fitted, cleaned, and ready for the show. But these costumes had been sitting in storage closets for God knew how long, and the smell of mothballs had permeated even the tiniest fibers. Feeling itchy already, I braced myself for the onslaught of stinky polyester.

"Here are the first ten," she said, depositing an armful of hangers onto the rack behind the screen. "Come out when you're ready and we'll work through them. I need to make notes and pin them if we decide they are winners."

I rounded the dressing screen, separating the garments so I could critique them. *No, this one has too much lace. Not this one either. Quinn would never wear burnt orange. Um, hell no—the only person who'd wear this one is Liberace.* My opinions didn't matter, though, so I tried each and every shirt on, playing Barbie as Melissa jotted things down on her notepad before pointing to the screen for the next one.

Pulling what felt like top number 328 over my head, I turned to the mirror to examine my appearance. For being petite, my curves were pretty awesome. My full B cups looked perky as hell in this blouse. The burgundy fabric complimented my skin and hair, casting a soft glow. Tiny pearlized buttons adorned the front, climbing from my navel to the top of my neck, ending just below my chin. I silently prayed to the theatre gods that this one made the cut for the show. Melissa's voice rang through the room, but with my head covered in fabric, I could only make out muffled words.

You know when you try on someone else's ring and it gets stuck on your finger? That instant feeling of panic and dread when you twist and pull to no avail?

Try it with a shirt that refuses to come off as easily as it went on.

Agitation and fear clouded my common sense as I grunted and tried to wrestle with the fabric. The buttons tugged at my hair, tangling together and making it impossible to remove the shirt myself. Why didn't I unfasten more buttons? With my arms straight over my head and my face covered, I stumbled blindly from behind the screen in defeat. I muttered in what I hoped was the direction of Melissa. "Mel, a little help, please?" I listened as footfalls echoed close to me, and I sighed in relief.

Warm hands relaxed my arms into a bent position. Pulling slowly, deft fingers worked the snarled buttons from my hair and I was freed from my cloth restraint. A relieved gulp of air made its way into my lungs while I focused my eyes on Melissa.

Wait, Melissa has boobs. There are no boobs on this person.

I was nose-to-chest with a plane of hard muscle covered in a gray raglan T-shirt.

Definitely not Melissa.

Bash crossed his arms in front of his chest as he took a small step back, his raised brow laser-beamed in on where my shirt should be. I traced his line of sight, my chin dipping lower.

Son of a motherbitch, I didn't have a bra on.

The shirt was thick enough that I didn't need one.

My hands flew to my bare chest, my forearms grasping for privacy as I squeaked out an embarrassed apology and explanation. Blood rushed to my face as I stood in front of Bash in all—well, half—of my glory. It wasn't like I'd flashed him on purpose, and even if I had, my equipment wasn't what got his motor running. Taking a deep breath, I cleared my throat and nudged him with my sock-covered foot. No way was I moving my arms. Bash stared for what felt like the longest two seconds of my life before averting his gaze and handing the crumpled shirt over.

"Don't worry, it's not like I haven't seen boobs before." He winked. "Nice shirt, though. Really brought out your...assets. I've gotta say, I think I like this au naturel look better than that blue lacy bra from your apartment."

A quick blush bloomed over my décolletage before annoyance and sexual frustration gripped inside my belly. Covering my boobs with the wrinkled shirt, I stepped forward and shoved him and his stupid muscles out of my changing area. He really needed to stop walking in on me with my tits out. It wasn't helping anyone.

"What are you doing here, ass?" I asked through the thin wall, fastening the clasp and adjusting the straps of my bra.

"I was coming in to try stuff on. But now, I'm much happier helping stuff come off." He laughed.

I pulled my flannel over my head and worked through the buttons. *Mental note—buttons are tiny circular assholes. Only buy things with Velcro or zippers from now on.*

"Fun fact, Callie; Bash and flash rhyme." The idiot started laughing even harder. "It's like we were meant to be."

I slipped on my Chucks and stepped out from behind the screen, only to find him doubled over against the mirror. "Did you really just say that?"

He leaned against the counter, hands in the front pockets of his jeans, a cocky grin on his face. The round lightbulbs surrounding the mirrors had given me multiple reflections of him at once, and I couldn't be mad about it. He looked beautiful. He looked happy. Moving my pseudo-glare back to him, I found him yet again having a staring contest with my boobs.

I think my boobs were losing.

I snapped my fingers, trying to break whatever secret bonding experience he seemed to be having with them.

"Hey! My face is up here. Bash. Bash! What color are my eyes?"

He looked up. "Um, 34C?"

I burst into laughter, wiping tears from my cheeks as he stood there stunned. I guess Bash could still appreciate a decent rack. Every time I looked at his face, I started cracking up again. His brow furrowed deeper, that bottom lip of his jutting out as I went to town.

Melissa walked back into the dressing room, her poor arms weighed down with piles of men's clothing. She looked back and forth between Bash and me, trying to figure out what had happened while she was gone.

"Um, I'm not even going to guess with you two. Weirdos," she muttered that last bit under her breath and heaved her pile of garments over the back of a chair. "Since you're here early, Bash, why don't you try these on?"

He took three hangers from her hands, his name

safety-pinned to the different colored dress shirts. Bash could have walked behind the screen, but I guess it was torture-Callie day. My jaw went slack when he reached behind his head and pulled, making quick work of the cotton covering his skin. Melissa and I were meager creatures that were now sucked into his devious strip show. We exchanged quick, wide-eyed glances as he tossed his T-shirt onto the counter before putting his toned biceps through the sleeves of a navy dress shirt. Bash smirked and I had a sudden need for a huge glass of water. He lazily worked the buttons, his focus more interested in my reaction. Was he trying to make this look like a striptease in reverse? Because it was working. I suddenly wished I had a wad of dollar bills in my back pocket.

I shook the thoughts from my brain. He totally knew he was pulling a Magic Mike.

What a tempting tease.

"Bash, go behind the freaking screen, for Christ's sake," I complained, gesturing to his exposed chest. "We don't need to see *all* of that."

Melissa started cackling, turning away to label more outfits.

He backed up slowly, a devious smile growing on his lips. "I just figured since I saw yours, it was only fair that I showed you mine."

I slapped my hand over my eyes at the very same time Melissa spun around and screamed, "What? Bash saw your boobs?"

He finished buttoning the shirt, obviously amused that I was fuming.

"It's not what you think, Mel," I explained. "The stupid buttons on that burgundy top got stuck in my hair and I thought it was you helping me get it off."

Bash walked forward, cutting between Mel and me. "It's okay, Melissa. I got it off, probably much quicker than she could have on her own."

I was going to kill him, or at the very least maim him. Her face was almost the color of that ill-fated shirt, her embarrassment at this situation looking like it was worse than my own. She was such a shy, sweet, almost-prudish person. I couldn't imagine what was going through her mind.

I swung him around, yanking the fabric surrounding his bicep, and dragged him behind the screen. I hit him as hard as I could in the shoulder, immediately shaking out the pain radiating from my knuckles. "What the hell are you made of, rock? You hurt my hand!" I whisper-shouted.

He looked gobsmacked. "I hurt you? *You* hit *me*! How is this my fault?" He lifted my hand, appraising the damage and rubbing his calloused thumb over my sore knuckles.

"I wouldn't have had to punch you if you didn't just embarrass me and Melissa like that!"

Bash kissed my swollen fist with a wink, which only angered me more. "Violence is not the answer, Calliope."

I murmured something foul under my breath before turning on my heels and storming away. Yelling toward the piles of clothes that I'm sure were suffocating my friend, I let Melissa know I was finished for the day.

Twenty-Three

I STOMPED OUT OF THE ROOM AND QUICKLY rushed up the stairs to the main floor, but the footfalls pounding behind me meant that Bash was on my heels. He reached for my elbow, gently pulling me backward. Thrown off guard at the reverse force, I panicked and missed the next step. I felt myself falling and squeezed my eyes shut, bracing for the painful impact of my ass against the hard floor. But it never came. Bash was quick, and before I knew what was happening, his arms were wrapped around my waist. My synapses fired on all cylinders when I realized I was safe—that once again, he saved me. He righted me, pulling me close enough that our bodies brushed together.

My hand didn't hurt anymore, but my ovaries were starting to.

He leaned closer, his magnetic force pulling me to him. Slipping the backpack from my shoulder, Bash wrapped his arms around my waist to tug me closer. My gaze settled on his plump lower lip, his teeth grazing over it back and forth.

He was thinking about it.

I bit my own, the pressure building in my core as Bash circled his thumbs into my lower back. He wanted to kiss me. I could see it. Feel it.

"Sweets..." he said huskily.

I was stock-still, too afraid to break the delicious tension swirling around us. I lifted my hands and skimmed over the rough denim until I reached his hipbones, until my fingers were tangled in the hem of his shirt, clinging, begging.

Sweet baby Jesus, please kiss me, Bash.

I licked my lips, leaning slightly into him as I closed my eyes. Finally. I held my breath and waited.

One second. One single second was all it took. One second to realize that I forgot myself.

That one stupid second where he remembered who he was about to kiss.

That one fucking second where we both realized I wasn't a guy and he released me.

My heart bottomed out as I shoved my hands in the back pockets of my jeans. He coughed to clear his throat, tugging at the long tendrils of hair on the top of his head. He was giving me whiplash with his mood swings.

"I'm, uh, going to have to buy you a bubble suit," he said, his focus on the wall above my head.

I rolled on the balls of my feet, fury and

embarrassment fighting its way through my limbs. I couldn't do this push-and-pull anymore. Stick a fucking fork in me, because I was done. Why did we keep playing this cat and mouse game? Why did I keep getting sucked in? A lump of humiliation formed in my throat and I knew I needed to say something to put a stop to it once and for all.

It was one thing to fool myself into letting the flirting and the touching happen—it was an entirely different being to allow it to mess with my head. The laugh that came bubbling from my throat was full of heartbreak and resentment.

"You should have just let me fall," I said, looking him straight in the eye, teeth clenched. "Might have been less painful than this."

He closed the distance between us and I halted him with my hand, slowing him from entering my personal space again. "Callie, I—"

"No. Just don't, Bash. I don't know why we keep playing these games...no, you know what? I'm not that girl—or that *person*, whatever—I'm not playing. I can't do this anymore." I don't know what he was thinking, but the vibe he'd given off was that of a guy about to kiss someone. Maybe he was questioning his sexual orientation, but if so, I wasn't the girl he could practice on until he figured it out. It was time to start putting myself first. Scooping my backpack from the floor, I hurled it over one shoulder. "I'm done. I'm leaving. Don't follow me."

I spun around and hurried up the remaining steps. His brow furrowed as I scolded him and his hand yanked at the strands of his hair until he looked less put-together than I felt. He was warring inside just as much as I was, but I couldn't afford to care anymore. It hurt too much. When I reached the top of the stairs, he called out my name.

"Are we okay?" he asked rigidly.

His fingers were clasped around the railing so hard, I could see the white of his knuckles from here. Pulling my flannel around my body tighter, I fought the chill running down over my skin that most certainly wasn't from a cold breeze.

Taking one last look at him, I adjusted my bag and blew out a breath. The dirty ceiling tiles were a welcome reprieve for my teary eyes. Anything was better than looking at him again.

"We will be. Just give me some time."

I wasn't sure if it was good or bad that she was gone, but the apartment and my mood seemed even sadder without Evie in it. She'd left this morning for Chicago to audition for a dance company and wouldn't be home for a few days. As much as I wanted my BFF with me, it was probably for the better that she was avoiding my dramatics.

My eyes were leaking that watery crap again. Why

is it that when you really *didn't* want to cry, tears were in an abundant supply? I wiped the salty streaks away with my damp sleeve and willed myself to stop. Bash had successfully screwed with me again, and it wasn't anyone's fault but my own. I felt like I'd just gone through a real breakup, which was pathetic since the last 'serious' boyfriend I had was for six months my senior year of high school. This hurt way more than that. After the first full night of wallowing—and an entire bag of cheese puffs—I had a slightly orange-tinted epiphany. I'd given myself a two-day grace period before I decided to put on my big-girl pants and get the hell over him once and for all.

For real this time.

Mind over matter, right? No one likes a pity party when they're the only one in attendance.

I shook the thoughts from my head as my phone vibrated next to me. Pulling in it front of my puffy eyes, I groaned when I saw it was yet another text from Tucker. *Give it a rest, man.* Flipping the button on the side to silent, I tossed it farther away from me on the couch, hitting my foot in the process.

I had managed to avoid at least a dozen phone calls and fifty texts between Tuck and *he-who-won't-be-named*, but it didn't stop them from irritating the crap out of me. Unless one of them was dying on the side of the road, nothing would break my grace-period-inspired moping.

I knew I was going to have to see them on campus

and during rehearsals, and I'd deal with that when it happened. It wasn't that I couldn't handle Tucker, it's just that I wasn't ready for the onslaught of accusatory questions about why I was being such a downer. So, avoidance? It was the best option. I'd rather remain holed up in my apartment with my carbs and greasy hair than try and people like a grown-up.

I shoved my hand back into the bag of Doritos on my lap, mindlessly watching a Kirsten Dunst romcom I loved as a teen. I scowled at her stupid face. I watched every single one of those movies when I was younger, and they were a bag of bullshit.

Young love didn't always end in a happily ever after. Sometimes it ended with wearing your fat pants and the delivery guy knowing your address by heart.

The screen on my phone illuminated the blanket surrounding it. "Oh my God, stop. I'm not going to answer you," I yelled at it. It didn't relent, so with a huff I grabbed it—with the plan to throw it across the room—when I saw it was a small photo of Tinder Jordan accompanied by a text notification.

Jordan: Hey, Callie! It's been a minute. How are u?

My thumb hovered over the unlock button. How was I? That was laughable.

I'm great, Tinder Boy. I fell for a gay guy and held onto my feelings for three years and now I'm a basket case. How are you?

Callie: Great. Just awesome. How are you?

Bashful

Jordan: Doing good, doing good.

I cringed at his lack of proper grammar. Everything was making me particularly cranky today. I'd blame it *all* on Bash, but I'm sure it had just as much to do with the cramps that decided to invade my uterus this morning.

Jordan: So there's this party at my frat next week. I'd really luv for u to come. I'd be honored if u would be my date. There's no French food, so don't worry about that. ;-)

I was fully aware that our first date was completely terrible. Horrific, basically, but I was a sucker for second chances. Jordan probably thought that taking a date to his parents' restaurant was a surefire way to impress someone, and with me it backfired. Who would I be hurting if I went out on a second date with him?

No one. Definitely not Bash.

I was serious about getting back into the dating pool, or at least the shallow end. Plus, at least going out again with Jordan meant I wouldn't have to log back into Tinder yet to search for another winner. I didn't think I had that in me. What happened to the meet-cutes at coffee shops? Was that all just a big conspiracy designed by Starbucks to sell more ventis? My fingers flew over the letters on my phone as I typed out my response.

Callie: As long as there's alcohol instead of food, I'm down. That sounds like fun. I'd love to. :-)

Jordan: U a party girl? I didn't picture that, but I'm liking it. I'll text u with the details?

Callie: It's a date.

Putz. I had a feeling I was going to regret this decision.

Twenty-Four

FULFILLING MY FORTY-EIGHT-HOUR PITY-PARTY goal—and after convincing Tucker to leave me alone by claiming cramps—I'd gone through the motions when class resumed on Monday. Evie had returned in the middle of the night on a red-eye, and was still sleeping when I'd left the apartment. Even though the October weather was colder than I'd like, I decided to forgo my car and had been walking to and from campus. Google said stress could be relieved by music and exercise, and maybe that was true—the walking helped with my anxiety, and the volume in my earbuds was high enough to dull my thoughts.

Pulling my beanie low over my unkempt hair, I fixed my gaze on the concrete at my feet.

A lot of students here had ugly shoes.

When I wasn't in class I kept my nose to the grindstone, filling all vacant hours with studying and polishing my lines for Playing with Fire. It kept my mind from wandering.

I'd barely survived rehearsals with Bash, putting on a brave face during our scenes and fading into the background as soon as Professor James called 'scene.' I'd sit in the unlit corner of the auditorium with my nose in my Kindle, far away from the rest of the cast. Everyone had sensed the mood shift in me—that or they were afraid of my newfound resting bitch face.

Bash's voice jarred me anytime it projected from the stage, halting my reading. I'd been reading the same page of my book for the last week. I felt a tinge of heartache when I looked at him, his body turned outward and his lines directed toward my side of the auditorium. I knew he was looking for me. Thankfully the spotlight blinded him.

When Professor James called rehearsal fifteen minutes early, I jumped from my seat. Throwing my bag over my shoulder, I skipped down the wide steps and pushed through the double doors before anyone else had even packed up their belongings.

Before I even heard the telltale *click* of the doors shutting, a palm landed on my shoulder. I spun around with closed eyes, bracing for it to be the one person I couldn't handle being around. I was *so* close to escaping unscathed.

Thank God. It's not Bash.

Tucker enveloped me in a hesitant hug, patting my back like an awkward uncle. "There, there, Calliope," he shushed, moving one hand to my hair.

I wriggled out of his grasp, the dirty look on my face enough to give him pause. "Not today, Satan."

Tucker lifted his arms in surrender, eyebrows high on his forehead. "Easy, tiger. I'm not going to grill you. I wanted to see how you've been. Everyone has been worried about you."

Yeah, *everyone* meaning his roommate. I loved Tucker, but that man would spill the tea for a Snickers bar. If I told him how I was feeling, I was pretty much telling Bash directly. Not happening.

"I'm fine, Tuck. Great, okay? I'm in a hurry, so if you want to keep talking then you'd better keep up." I pivoted on my heels without looking back and listened to the rustling of his peacoat as he trailed behind me.

Catching up, he matched my stride, the click of his dress shoes pattering on the sidewalk.

"To risk sounding like a campus counselor—it's okay not to be okay," he murmured through one side of his upturned mouth, brushing my shoulder with his own. I stopped in my tracks and turned to face him. Lifting my hand, I cooled my features before yanking him roughly by his bowtie down to my level.

"Tucker Garrison, I swear to God, if you don't shut up, I'm going to tell the whole school about the time you sharted freshman year."

His eyes went wide, bulging out of his head like one of those rubber squeeze toys.

"You wouldn't."

"Try me."

Tucker paled at my raised eyebrow. He focused on my don't-test-me expression, knowing full well not to test me. Unfortunately for him, I'd gotten my stubbornness from both parents—if I said something, I meant it. Not breaking eye contact, I released the tie and he righted himself, the color in his cheeks rushing back. Adjusting his tie, he held up his pinky.

"Fine. But I don't like it. He may be my bestie, but you are too."

I gripped his pinky with my own and huffed.

"I know, Tuck. Just drop it, okay? Nothing is going to change between you and me. I just need a break from all of *that*," I said, gesturing wildly in the air. I had to freaking spell it out for Tucker. "Let's talk about you, instead. How's Harold? Good?"

His puzzled expression confused me before his face lit up in recognition. "Harold? Oh, girl, that was just a one-and-done. And trust me, it wasn't anything to write home about. His dick was so small he could fuck a cheerio. Like for real, it looked like—"

I slapped my hand over his mouth, cringing. Ooookay. Hearing about his one-night stand's peen was a topic I didn't want festering in my brain for years to come. "Nope. Stop right there," I said, holding my fingers against his lips while he mumbled beneath them.

While I could usually handle Tuck in much larger doses, my absence had made him excited to share too much, too quickly. Giving him a quick hug goodbye, I headed to Loxley's for a Happy Hour drink.

Bashful

⟶

I dropped my jacket and book bag into the backseat of my car before walking briskly into the bar, staring at the neon sign. Evie was meeting me up here, and I was thankful for it. I was feeling pathetic enough, I didn't need to drink alone on top of it.

Pulling the door open, the telltale aroma of grease and beer invaded my senses. Doing a quick assessment of the room, I noted an unfamiliar band setting up on the stage as I took my time heading to the bar. Evie was already here, talking to the bartender animatedly. Plopping onto the stool next to her, I rubbed my tired eyes before bumping her shoulder in greeting.

Tracing her finger along the rim of her nearly-empty drink, she batted her long eyelashes at the man behind the bar before turning to give me a quick peck on the cheek.

"Hello, love. This is Garrett. Garrett, Callie," she swooned.

What the hell? I'd never seen her so smitten. I gave him a quick nod before turning back to Evie with a puzzled expression.

"He's just started," she explained to me. She grabbed my knee under the bar, where Garrett couldn't see and squeezed hard enough that a small yelp escaped from my lips. It was a little overenthusiastic—I'm sure there'd be a bruise tomorrow—but that squeeze was a surefire sign that she was excited. Evie turned on her sultry voice like it was a switch and lowered her chin. "Garrett, would you mind terribly if I asked you to make us both a Long Island?"

He stood a bit taller, puffing out his chest as a grin overtook his face before he cleared her glass from the counter. "Can do, beautiful."

Evie stretched over the teak of the bar top and blatantly checked out his ass when he turned around to set up our drinks. I watched as he poured various alcohols into the tall glasses, appreciative that he was making them stronger than usual. While he was distracted, Evie slyly produced a rhinestone-covered compact mirror from her purse and checked her makeup. Rolling bright red gloss over her full lips, she smacked them before whispering to me.

"Look at that arse, Callie. It's so perfect. I want to bite it," she gushed, putting her fists to her chin and staring again.

I did a quick butt-check before watching him add the final splash of soda to our glasses and wedging a lemon on each rim. Nice ass be damned, he needed further study before I deemed him worthy of my best friend's affection. He was attractive in a biker-gang kind of way, which wasn't my taste—or Evie's. His wavy light-brown hair was pulled to the crown of his head into a rough man-bun that matched his lengthy, albeit groomed, beard. A dark T-shirt with the Loxley's emblem on his chest writhed and flexed as he moved, tattoos peeking out from the edges of the tight sleeves.

His attractiveness matched my best friend's, so he had that going for him. Plus, Evie had a heart-on for him, so he must've said something right. I silently nodded my approval, while also making a mental reminder to run a background check on him later.

"Get him, girlfriend. You know you want to," I said, pulling my phone from my purse while she eye-fucked him. "He seems pretty damn smitten already." I laughed.

"He's giving me a lady boner. All my Brit-bits are tingling."

We giggled as Garrett came back with our drinks, his attention solely focused on Evie.

"On the house." He winked.

I'm pretty sure Evie floated into la-la land after that, because I couldn't keep her attention. I'd lost her for the night.

As happy as it made me to see her finally interested in someone, I couldn't help but feel a dull sting in my heart. Evie was more deserving of love than anyone I knew, and maybe Garrett would be her Prince Charming.

That gave me a sliver of hope.

Maybe that hope was for the pain to disappear instead of taking permanent residence in my gut. Maybe that hope was for a Hemsworth to walk through the door and sweep me off my feet. Maybe that hope was to cut my losses now and become the Guinness World Record holder as the youngest ever spinster cat lady. I knew one thing, though—whatever that little sliver was, I was happy it was there.

Leave it to a bearded biker and a bubbly Brit to restore my faith in love at first sight.

I swirled my straw slowly, watching the condensation roll down the glass to the soggy napkin underneath. The alcohol was quickly warming my belly, a welcome distraction from the flirting going on next to me. Turning to Evie, I excused myself from their conversation before snatching my belongings and moving closer to the band. I found a small table near the wall, draped in shadow. Perfect.

A halo of light surrounded the lead singer. He tapped the microphone in front of him with a black-polish-covered fingernail, testing the sound as a small crowd gathered. His hair was long, the dark stringy curls tied at the nape of his neck. He looked like he needed a shower, or possibly ten. Maybe everyone in the front would inhale and pass out on the floor before he could even start singing.

"Hey, guys, we are The Addison. Thanks for coming tonight. We hope you enjoy the show."

Deep booms from the drummer echoed around the room as the bassist joined in on the downbeat. I watched each musician move their fingers deftly, studying their body language while I swayed in my seat with the rhythm. It was a rock song, something I normally didn't get into, but it was catchy as hell. GreasyPants—I mean, the lead singer—had a smooth, low tenor to his voice.

His fingers were pliable on the strings of his guitar, the expertise of his crafts impressive. I watched from the sidelines, noting the crowd had grown exponentially in a short amount of time. I pulled out my phone and looked them up on social media, reminding myself to download some of their songs later.

"This next one goes out to all the heartbreakers," GreasyPants called out, his lips close to the mic.

I stiffened in my seat as he sang through the verses, the chorus piercing me like a thousand knives.

Floated like a feather
drifting in my air
pushing souls together
moving into me
then you flew away
then you flew away
my heart was your cage
never mine at all
the bars are mine to bear now
spread your wings and let me fall

The crowd erupted in cheers as the last notes faded away, the noise deafening. Sniffling, I blinked back tears from the corners of my eyes. Every emotion that dripped from his voice, every word escaping his lips soaked in that gut-wrenching pain—I felt it. He looked drained, like the words took every ounce of energy his body had to offer.

He had been broken and bled through it onstage.

If he could lay it all out there, performing through his pain night after night, then I could get through the rest of my show with Bash.

I could heal too, though I might break a little bit more in the process.

But that was okay.

I stood and nodded to the singer as his eyes caught mine, saluting him in solidarity before walking away.

I hoped whoever the girl who hurt him was got crotch scabies.

Team GreasyPants for the win.

Twenty-Five

PLASTIC RED CUPS LITTERED EVERY AVAILABLE surface as Jordan and I arrived at his frat party. He wrapped an arm around my shoulders, nodding a greeting to some and pounding his fist with others. Sound blasted from the speakers in each corner of the living room, all held up by duct tape. *Seemed safe.* I steered Jordan in the direction of the kitchen with a turn of my hips—anything to escape imminent death-by-stereo equipment.

He lowered his mouth to my ear, his breath tickling my skin. "Are you ready for a drink, gorgeous?" he asked over the music, careful not to deafen me by shouting. I nodded, pointing questionably to the liquor bottles and mixers on the laminate counter near the back door. Jordan grinned, grabbing my hand to take me to the good stuff.

"Normally, this is reserved for girlfriends, you know," he said playfully as he splashed cranberry juice over the icy vodka. "But you're a girl, and I consider you more than a friend." He winked. "I think we can get away with it."

Smirking, I accepted the cup from his hands and took a sip. Damn, he made it strong. Not that I'd complain—it was a thousand times better than drinking the lukewarm, watery gnat-piss these guys considered beer. Before he could turn back to make himself a drink, a whoosh of air flew past my head. Above me, a hairy fist shot out to meet with Jordan's. He spun me around, and I lifted my eyes higher and higher to the behemoth standing in front of me.

"Rich, Callie. Callie, this is Rich." He gestured between us.

I stuck my hand out and up, unable to blink. This guy must have been at least six foot seven and three hundred fifty pounds. He returned with his own mammoth paw, wrapping it around not just my hand, but half of my forearm.

"The liquor is for girlfriends only, Jordy. Not some groupie," he softly yelled, as if his height meant that I was out of earshot.

What an asshole. I'd never be a groupie. I'd tell him to go suck it, but I'm sure that was a groupie's job.

"Rich, huh? Can I call you Richard? Or should I just settle on calling you Dick? Seems appropriate."

At that very moment, two songs shifted from one to the other in a silent transition. My words echoed throughout the room, reverberating off the walls. Jaws dropped around us and everyone froze.

Rich threw his head back and laughed voraciously, and I could swear the entire kitchen let out a collective sigh. As the music picked back up, a song about apple-bottom jeans started blaring through the enclosed space.

The big man slapped Jordan on the back before wiping tears from his eyes. "Keep this half-pint around, will ya, Jordy? I like her." He picked up two forty-ounce beers in his giant fists before stomping away.

"Holy shit, Callie," Jordan said, looking at me like I'd just won the lottery.

"I'm so sorry, it just came out. He *was* being a dick, calling me a groupie like that. I'm sorry." Defending my actions to *Jordy* was frustrating, especially when I didn't feel the need to apologize.

"I've never seen anyone talk like that to Rich. Everyone's terrified of him," he explained. "Sorry for not jumping in. I was mentally preparing to get my ass kicked."

"For what?"

"For defending my girl," he stated matter-of-factly. "You are one of a kind, Callie. You just charmed the crap out of the scariest guy on campus like it was nothing. I'm terrified what you'll do to me."

I'm not your girl.

I shrugged at Jordan with a small smirk, unsure how to respond. With his hand on the small of my back, he guided me through the back door, which led to a screen-covered porch. Large vintage bulbs were strung along the ceiling, highlighting a group of guys playing beer pong. The 'table' they constructed was slightly terrifying—a giant piece of plywood held up by what appeared to be a broken bookcase. Jordan greeted some of the people closest to us while I hung back and took in the rest of the space. Decaying paint was peeling from the beams, and small tears in the screen were allowing in the last of the autumn's mosquitos.

Shouts of victory came from the other side of the porch, the drunken victors temporarily overshadowing the booming bass of the music. Behind them, high-pitched shrieks came from girls who'd been sitting on the laps of guys clad in polo shirts with popped collars. I didn't know how they weren't freezing, their short skirts teetering close to showing off the goods.

Ah, those must've been the groupies Rich the dick was referring to.

"Do you want to play next?" Jordan asked, gesturing to the game.

I stepped forward, anxiously aware of the multiple sets of eyes waiting for my answer. The whorebags in the corner were whispering to each other, making it all too obvious that I was the topic of discussion.

"She's dressed like a snobby sorostitute," the fake blonde said, loud enough that she wanted me to hear.

Good one, Barbie. "Excuse me?"

I'd been here for all of ten minutes, and I'd been insulted twice. I got that a fraternity party wasn't my scene, but I didn't stick out like a sore thumb. I stepped ahead of Jordan, challenging her with a raised eyebrow to say something, anything else. I was feeling feisty tonight. She backed down, slinking into her flavor of the night and guzzling a Smirnoff Ice.

Looking down at my clothes, I didn't feel embarrassed by my appearance. My pink V-neck sweater was just low enough to show off a bit of the girls, and my distressed gray skinny jeans and fringy booties completed the cozy-cute fall look I was going for. Miniskirts weren't my style, and while I wasn't usually one to judge, it was hard to keep my snark at bay when I saw their teeth chattering. That's what they get for being bitches—and for wearing tank tops in near-freezing temperatures.

Whatever. Sweaters are for winners.

I didn't need some random guy's lap to keep me warm.

I turned to Jordan, who wore a mask of indifference. "I'm going to go find the bathroom. I need to wash my hands before I catch some weird skank-to-air disease. Next game?"

"No worries. Up the stairs and to your right, babe," he said with a smirk before turning around and joining in on the laughter from the group.

Thanks for defending my honor, by the way. 0 for two, Jordan. 0. For. Two.

Weaving my way through the crowd had proven to be more difficult than I planned. I was drenched in sweat and drips of stale beer by the time I reached the upstairs bathroom. At least it was vacant. Huffing out a breath, I closed myself in and turned the brass lock before banging the back of my head against the door. I'd sink into a pile on the floor, but come on—this was a fraternity house. I should've brought one of those bodily-fluid black lights. I gripped my phone tightly and sent a message.

Callie: Thank you for never letting me rush or become a sorostitute. I now owe you money.

Minutes later, Evie still hadn't responded. She'd texted earlier about a last-minute date with Garrett, so I wasn't expecting anything in return. I glanced down at the time—only 10:00. Hurling myself into the dating world was still happening, regardless of my shitty luck so far. No going home yet.

I'd give this date a little while longer, so I had no choice but to brave the crowd once again. Washing my hands thoroughly, I left the bathroom and made my way back to Jordan.

My quest had failed. The beer pong idiots were so wasted they were no help in locating their own asses, let alone Jordan. I scanned each room, eyes roaming as quickly as they could for any sign of him, my tiptoes not much help. I wished I would've known at least one other person at this party. The buddy system made complete sense now.

I shot off a quick text once I reached the front door,

letting him know I'd meet him outside on the porch when he could find me.

The cold night air was a reprieve for my desperate lungs. I breathed in heavily before scrunching up my face, contorting my forehead as I sought out the very obvious smell invading my nostrils. Although in decay, the fraternity had a wraparound front porch that went around both sides. Moving to the right, the skunky smell grew more powerful as I rounded the corner.

Void of light, the darkest recess was filled with a small circle of people, smoke billowing above them. Puffs and giggles surrounded me as I moved forward and found Jordan near the back.

"Hey, babe, there you are," he greeted cloudily, breaking from the circle, his last hit still in his mouth.

Yeah, I'm so not your babe. I was pretty sure he'd completely forgotten about bringing me here until now.

"Want some?"

I cringed. I'd smoked pot before, but I really believed it was enjoyable because of the company you were with, not just how it made you feel. The fact that Jordan had ditched me—on a second date that *he* sought out—had put me off from this entire night.

"No, I'm good. Thanks."

"More for me," he said, his eyes bloodshot.

I'd had enough. I'd rather be single than deal with moronic douchebags.

"Look, Jordan, you're a really nice guy, but this isn't working for me. I'm going to go."

He slowly flicked his eyes between the group and me, finally deciding it was worth losing the last toke to offer me a ride home. My thanks-but-no-thanks was countered with, "at least let me get you an Uber."

Ever the gentleman.

He tried to walk me down to the sidewalk in his last-ditch effort to gain a little repoire—and maybe a kiss good night. "Hey, Callie? Next time a guy asks you out, try removing the stick from your ass before you go."

Oh, fuck no.

"Next time you see your mom, let her know that her precious old French lady thought she was an actual prostitute!"

With a boisterous wave, I blew a kiss at his shocked face and hopped in the cheap SUV that pulled up to the curb and slammed the door without a second glance. I quickly lifted off the seat just enough to grab my phone from my butt pocket, angrily uninstalling Tinder from my apps. No dates were better than shitty dates, and Jordan was a big steamy pile of the stuff.

Twenty-Six

DATING WAS OFF THE TABLE FOR NOW, AND MY classwork was showing it. It had been two weeks since I'd spoken to Bash outside of our scene work. Okay, it'd been two weeks since I'd spoken to anyone really, besides Evie, and I was finally getting to a place where I was fine with being alone. I managed to pull on my big-girl pants so high I probably had a camel toe, but I *did it*. I was proud of myself.

I readied myself for the next five days. Technically, it was "Tech Week," but the only person who called it that was Professor James. As actors, we called it Hell Week—the calm before the storm. It was when all of the technical elements—costumes, sound, lighting, makeup, the whole shebang—were run through and fine-tuned before we had an audience. I knew it would be grueling. We'd go through the show two or three times each night in full costume and makeup, sweating our asses off under the hot lights in order to get out all the kinks. At the end of the week, we'd have two final dress rehearsals, finely polishing our characters without interruption before the opening on Friday night.

Throwing my navy cheerleading duffel from high school onto the bed—yes, I still used it as that bad boy was DURABLE—I made a mental list of all the things I needed to pack for the dressing room. Throwing in two sticks of deodorant and a few comfy outfits, I made my way to the bathroom. Grabbing my hairbrush and tucking a sandwich bag full of eight million bobby pins into the side pocket, I picked up my slippers near the door before heading to the kitchen for some snacks.

Once my bag was stuffed to the brim with carbs, extra water, and energy drinks, I hitched the bag over my shoulder and grunted at the weight. Smiling at the fridge pad, I scribbled a quick note to Evie reminding her I'd be dead on my feet when I got home. There was a 90-percent probability I'd see that note again before she did. That girl was head over heels in insta-love with her bartender boyfriend. Yeah, my Evie, who never spent more than a night with a guy, was calling him her *boyfriend*.

She'd been spending more time at his place than at our own, and it was a little lonely. She must've been having some killer honeymoon-phase sexy times with him considering she'd basically ghosted me. Luckily jealousy wasn't a thing in our friendship, or I might be turning greener than the hulk. My lady bits were drying up while hers were, well, the opposite.

It wasn't like I chose the no-sex life. The no-sex life chose me.

Born-again virgin? Not by choice. I was revirginating—that sounded better.

Melissa was stitching a hem when I walked in the dressing room, so I said a quick hello before casually dropping my duffel in the small cube that had my character's name on it. We each had the small space for our costume accessories, and we stashed personal belongings in there during showtime. Half of them usually held a flask, too.

I greeted Tess, our makeup captain, before sitting at the mirrors to examine my cosmetic sheet. An 8x10 photo of my face was taped to the corner of the mirror, a clear plastic overlay detailing the colors and shades I was to wear for the show.

"Shit, I forgot to grab wipes," I mumbled. Stage makeup was thick, meant to withhold hours of hot lighting and sweat. I bought foam makeup sponges in bulk because after one application, the poor thing was torn to shreds.

Tess appeared like a genie, holding out a pack in front of me. "Guard them with your life, woman. I only bought a few extras." She handed me a sharpie so I could scribble ownership on the packaging.

"Marry me," I said, blowing her air kisses.

"Sorry, love, but I'm kind of smitten already," she whispered, flitting her eyes to Melissa.

"Really?" I asked, completely shocked. I had no idea they were together. My Gaydar must be seriously off. "Is it serious?"

She smiled lovingly at Mel, who blushed before quickly getting back to her sewing. "It's definitely headed that way, I think," she said. "For as quiet as she is around here, she's a freaking lion in the bedroom."

Did I have "tell me about your sex life" tattooed on my forehead? Why did everyone feel the need to tell me these things? Maybe they could smell the desperation on me.

Laughing, I gave her a quick hug and congratulations before turning back to the mirror and grabbing a cleansing wipe.

Cleaning my face of my 'street makeup' left me bare to the world. My hands reached for my cheeks and dragged down, emphasizing the dark circles under my eyes. They would only get worse this week. I needed to find another way to rally besides overdosing on caffeine or skipping class in lieu of naps. Evie suggested that we have a girls' day soon, full of massages and highlights and pedicures—but that was going to have to wait until Hell Week was over.

The rest of the girls in the cast filed in, each one in a stage of makeup or hair for primary approval tonight. I was thankful that we didn't need to don our costumes too. Mine consisted of multiple changes, and while I'd practiced with Melissa, I had yet to do it while we were being timed for the show's length. We couldn't be longer than two hours including intermission. When I did the math, that meant I needed to be out of one outfit and into a new one within three minutes when I was offstage. A member of the costume crew would always be waiting behind the set, everything unbuttoned and unzipped, but I was still worried.

When I finished my face and hair, I cleaned up my station and moved closer to Mel.

"Hey, how much do you love me?" I asked.

I was met with squinted eyes.

"I feel like this is a trick question," she replied as she concentrated again on ironing a pair of men's pants. "I could say I love you a lot, but then you'd probably ask me for a kidney or something."

"No, not a kidney—I just—can you stay and time my outfit changes after rehearsal tonight? I want to try and get each act done in ten minutes if I can." I wasn't above begging, and if she said no, I'd bribe her.

Melissa set down the iron, the steam rising into the air. "I wish I could, but Tess and I are going out tonight. It's our six-month anniversary," she said, somehow happy and apologetic at the same time.

"Oh, that's okay, I'll figure something out," I replied, while mentally figuring out how to do it myself. Maybe if I had each outfit in a pile ready to go, it'd be possible.

"No, stop that," she said. "I can see the panic in your eyes. I don't want to get a reaming from Professor

James any more than you do if you can't make those changes on time. I'll find someone to do it with you. Just hang out in here after rehearsal is over and I'll make sure someone is here to help."

I bum-rushed her, thankfully evading the ironing board and potential third-degree burns. Hugging her tightly, I thanked her before heading for the auditorium.

Twenty-Seven

THE RUN-THROUGH WENT AS I EXPECTED IT would. Professor James stopped us every five minutes, eviscerating our confidence with his 'critiques.' That was par for the course at this point, with the exception that he was more of a dick than an average director. It was dark by the time we finished the first go-around, and James' face had turned a shade of red that made it look like his head would explode at any second. We were all sweaty, frustrated, and borderline hangry, so he dismissed us before we could run through the show a second time.

Luckily, that meant I wouldn't feel rushed timing my outfit changes. Maybe since we finished early, Melissa would be hanging around a bit longer and could help me instead of whoever she had found. I didn't know the younger crew members, and I wasn't too excited about the potential of them accidentally copping a feel during the flurry of fabric.

Mel rushed down the hall as I rounded the corner from the stairwell.

"Went well, huh?" she asked.

Rolling my eyes, I scoffed. "About as well as stepping on Legos while on a treadmill. So, can you stay for a little bit and help? I know you said you ladies were going out later, but—"

"Uh, we're going to go see a movie before dinner now. Something romantic and cheesy, the perfect kind of make-out movie," she squealed. "Don't worry, though, I got someone to help you. They should be here in a little bit!" Giving my shoulder a squeeze, she ran up the stairs with a smile on her face.

I moved to the dressing room, rifling through my bag for a granola bar. I chewed slowly, calming my growling stomach. I was going to have a date tonight, too; mine was just with my DVR and an unopened bag of Twizzlers I'd hidden from Evie. Throwing my wrapper in the garbage, I transferred my hangers to a smaller clothing rack and began unbuttoning.

Everyone around me was falling in love. I couldn't help but notice that people in love acted like a different version of themselves—giggly, aloof extensions of who they were before. Maybe love and stupidity went hand in hand. If that was the case, I did enough stupid things on my own. Maybe it was good that I hadn't truly fallen in love yet.

As I finished unzipping the last skirt, a knock rapped on the door and I swung around to greet my helper.

Practically doing a full spin, I was back around facing the clothes, sorting, doing anything to keep my hands busy.

"Hey, Melissa mentioned to the crew that you needed someone to help with your changes, but no one spoke up. I hope it's okay that I volunteered," Bash said, his deep timbre sending a shiver down my spine. He set his arm above his head on the doorframe, his stupid face smirking straight at me. "Plus, I've been told I'm good at quickly taking clothes off."

This was the first time we'd spoken offstage in weeks. The first time we'd been alone in weeks. No. Nope. I wasn't going back again.

I'd fought through my cravings for Chet's and the diner, too afraid with my luck that Bash would be there at the same time. That was hard enough. He would've sat me down and made me talk, find a way to weasel back in and break my walls down again.

Make me feel special again.

We'd laugh, he'd have his hooks back in, and I'd be right back where I started. I was an addict, and the only way to kick that craving was to quit Bash cold turkey. I couldn't crack now, not when I was so close.

"Callie, please talk to me. I don't want to play games either." He sighed. He looked devastated, his reflection mirroring my own. He ran his fingers through his tousled hair as he swayed from side to side, unsure if he should come closer.

I pulled a dress off the first hanger, the delicate cloth

falling into my lap. Rubbing the silk between my fingers, I chanced a peek at him before I spoke.

"I said we'd be okay, Bash. But there's no time limit for when that will be. Please don't force it." An ugly pit formed in my stomach. Did I mean what I was saying? Worry was an ugly bitch. I didn't want this nagging, unrequited love hanging over our friendship.

"For tonight, I hope you're really here to help. And the only talking should be about how fast I can go from this silk dress to that pantsuit."

His shoulders fell, not in defeat, but in understanding. Pulling his cell from his pocket, he tapped a few buttons and showed me the timer on the screen.

"Let's do this. How much time do you need?"

I don't know, Bash. I'll let you know when I figure it out.

Twenty-Eight

I SURVIVED. HELL WEEK WAS EXACTLY THAT—A swirling, fiery inferno completed by despair and self-doubt. Luckily, all the yelling and swearing had transformed Playing with Fire into something we were all proud of. It was our first night, and we were ready to perform.

Seated at the bulb-lit mirror in front of me, I appraised my face and hair. My dirty blond locks were pinned and rolled back at the crown of my head, sprayed stiff into a vintage coif. Heavy cake foundation had been contoured and rouged extensively to make my bone structure pop under the harsh lighting. My favorite part of my transformation was my eyes, though, the heavy black liner swept in a clean arch, causing my olive irises to shine.

Everyone in the dressing room quieted as "fifteen minutes to curtain," rang through the small round speaker in the ceiling. I popped up from my seat and wriggled into my first costume, the cool fabric a reprieve from the anxiety sweats that had taken up residence in my body. With one last look in the mirror, I touched up my dark lipstick and went upstairs.

After double-checking that my other costume changes were hung just offstage, I edged toward the curtain. Clutching the ropes that pulled the heavy velvet fabric apart, I snuck a glance at the audience. It was wrong to do, especially as a professional grown-up adult, but I still did it before every opening night no matter how old I got.

It was a full house, each seat sold out and occupied. Parents, students, and families whispered to each other before the lights dimmed, their excitement palpable. I spotted Evie in the third row, giggling as Garrett whispered in her ear from the seat next to her. My parents weren't coming until tomorrow night, which was fine. Having Evie here was enough pressure. She caught me late last night, pacing my room and going over a monologue, and comforted me. Before I left tonight, she insisted she'd be there. "Not having someone to root for you on opening night is just as bad as saying 'good luck' instead of 'break a leg,'" she'd said.

I wasn't one to challenge her crazy superstitions, but I was pretty sure those two would cancel each other out. Either way, I was happy to have someone in my corner rooting for me.

Moving into my position on stage, I felt him before I saw him. The lights were off, save for the stage crew's small flashlights checking the props and the set one last time.

"Two minutes to curtain," the stage manager whisper-hissed, and I let out a slow exhale.

Bash stood inches from my face, his minty breath tickling my skin. "Having butterflies, Sweets? I'm anxious, too."

"I'm not anxious," I muttered, my foot tapping the floor. "I'm just extremely well-aware of how many catastrophes could happen in the next two hours."

His quiet, throaty laugh appeased my nerves a little. If I was honest, though, the butterflies usually only lasted a few minutes into the performance, and then my confidence usually took over. Except this time.

All week, they never disappeared during the course of the run-throughs. Not once, not when Bash was so physically close. Even pretending to be someone else wouldn't convince those asshole butterflies to leave the pit of my stomach.

Stupid feelings. Stupid caterpillars and their giant dreams.

Bash stared down at me, and even in the dimness of the stage I could see his eyes sparkling.

"You're an amazing actress, Callie. I wouldn't be up here right now if it wasn't for you," he whispered, cupping my jaw with his hand. He rubbed his thumb back and forth over the seam of my bottom lip before he spoke again. "Do exactly what you told me that first night at the Black Box. Strip it all away and just put it yourself out there."

The knots in my stomach loosened slightly as he pulled away, both of us focused on the small gap at the bottom of the curtains. The house lights were lowering, the whispers of the audience quieting until all we heard were our own breaths.

Before the curtain rose, Bash smirked, whispering one last thing.

"We finally get to kiss tonight. I hope it doesn't suck."

In the few precious seconds we had before the curtain went up, my brain worked in triple time to figure out how I forgot that little detail until now. In the time before the lights blinded me, all I'd settled on was that maybe I'd been too distracted to even think about the kiss.

Or maybe, just maybe, I'd gotten over him enough that the thought of his lips on mine didn't freak me out anymore.

Bash faced me, speaking the first line, aware that this scene set the feel for how the rest of opening night would go. That sparkle hadn't left his eyes, his confidence oozing as he crossed to stage right. I squinted at him, thankful that Quinn was supposed to be angry.

He had to have been waiting until right before the lights went up to mention the kiss. *Bastard.* He wanted the last and *only* word on the subject. Throw me off my game.

He hopes it doesn't suck.

I really shouldn't play into this shit, but if he wanted

to play games again, that was fine. I could, too. We'd finally get to kiss tonight, and I'd make sure my lips shut his up on the subject once and for all.

The only thing that would suck was having to pretend not to like it.

"My burns hurt. Your scars won't fade. But we made it through the flames together, Quinn. We clawed and scratched our way out of the past. Forget about our families, our jobs, our lives before. Let's stop playing with fire and let the heat consume us both."

Bash reached over to me, his grip fisting the hair at the nape of my neck as he roughly joined my body with his.

"Let it burn," he whispered, his voice slightly cheating out to the audience. He cupped my face, my body on fire as his eyes closed.

My left arm snaked around his neck, my right splayed over his heart. I felt the rapid succession of beats as I prepared to make the move I'd been planning since intermission. He wanted a first kiss, wanted to joke about it like it was nothing.

I recited the final line, a small smirk gracing my lips. *"Let it burn."*

It was time for the stage kiss that was expected from the cast and crew, Bash included. A stage kiss convinced the audience that the actors were actually kissing, but in reality, it was just plastic movements and strategic head turns.

Ignoring the rules, I squeezed the back of his neck and went for it—the real deal.

I varied the pressure of my kiss, sucking gently on his lower lip. Frozen in place—probably in shock—Bash let me kiss him, giving just enough back that the audience got what they came for. Desire pooled in my stomach as I cheated us away from the crowd, teasing and coaxing the seam of his lips to let me in. The lights went out, applause deafening around us as the curtains lowered.

It was supposed to be payback for his comment before the show.

It wasn't.

Desperation coursed through me, hoping and praying that my kiss would have magical turn-him-straight superpowers. I knew this moment was fleeting—probably the only chance I'd ever have to kiss Bash this way.

I lifted the arches of my feet, getting closer, taking my one and only chance. I needed him to wake up.

Kiss me back.

My lids fluttered open, and even in the minimal light, his emerald irises made me want to melt into a puddle. He pulled back from me, his chest heaving as he unthreaded his fingers from my hair. My heart dropped, worried I'd crossed the line.

Again.

I didn't have time to worry about it.

Bash charged at me, his large hands cupping the sides of my face as he crashed his mouth against mine. He matched my kisses with the force of a thousand more, claiming my mouth like I belonged to him. My hands lowered, squeezing the hard muscles in his back through his dress shirt. He let out a soft groan, the hum of his voice sending shockwaves to my core.

"We did it!" "That was amazing!" The voices grew closer, the vibration of footsteps rumbling on the floor below us.

Bash traced my jaw with his thumb, his shoulders moving up and down as rapidly as his breaths. I felt an instant loss as he stepped backward, putting space between us as the backstage lights turned on. The cast and crew swallowed us in a frenzy, preparing for the curtain call. I couldn't catch my breath.

Bash was staring at me like he wanted to kill me.

He was pissed at me. I took it too far. *Fuck*. I needed to lighten the situation, remedy it with comedy. If that didn't work, I'd settle for groveling at his feet.

"You're lucky I didn't eat garlic first, Sebastian," I shouted, praying that my makeup covered the immense blush that had taken over my face and chest.

A few chuckles came from the crew that divided us, pulling props and set pieces out of the way. Bash shook his head, no smirk, no nothing before turning to line up in the eaves.

Guess I'd better brush up on my groveling.

LO BRYNOLF

Twenty-Nine

CHATTER FILLED THE LOBBY OF THE AUDITORIUM as friends and family congregated. They milled about drinking Styrofoam cups of complimentary coffee while they waited with flowers in their arms for their actors to emerge from the dressing rooms.

I rounded the corner, lifting to my tiptoes so I could scan over the crowd for Evie and Garrett.

"CALLIE!" Evie screamed, pushing her way through a group of students.

"Bloody hell, you were absolutely brilliant!" She beamed, squeezing me into her lithe frame. She kissed both of my cheeks before shouting, "Everyone! My best friend is going to be famous!"

I rolled my eyes over to Garrett, begging him to rescue me from her humiliation. He cleared his gruff throat and I pulled myself from her arms to accept the bouquet of gerbera daisies he'd been holding.

"That was some play, Callie. Really, you were

amazing. These are for you," he said, running a hand over his beard.

"From both of us," my best friend squealed. "Garrett, love, will you please go grab our jackets from coat check? I want to have a quick chat with this one before we head out."

He nodded, kissing her cheek and congratulating me once more before walking to the opposite end of the lobby. I was more than aware that Evie was going to drill me about that kiss, but I had hoped she'd let it sink in before she pushed for details. She linked her arm in mine, guiding us to a less populated area of the room. When she settled on a spot, she removed her arm from mine and pinched me.

"Ow, what the hell, E!"

Her ecstatic expression from seconds ago was gone, replaced with her Brit-Brat one. I rubbed at the sore spot on my arm, a frown on my face.

"No. What the hell, *you*, Callie. What did I just witness? Did you seriously just make out with Bash in front of three hundred people?" Her eyes were wild as she half-whispered, half-shrieked. "Why didn't you tell me that you moved past Mission: Eye-Fuck and worked your way up to Operation: Mouth-Assault? How long have you two been snogging?"

I massaged my temples, the adrenaline from the show and the kiss seeping out of my body. "It was just a joke, Evie. He told me right before the curtain went up that since it was our first kiss, that it was going to suck.

I was teaching him a lesson, that's it."

Evie narrowed her gaze, her left eyebrow arching high. She knew I was full of crap. I swear, she had the nose of a bloodhound—she could smell bullshit through the wind twenty miles away. For an actress, I really sucked at lying to those closest to me.

I fidgeted in my spot, debating whether or not I could make a mad dash away from her. Best-case scenario, I'd escape and she'd get distracted by Garrett and I could go home and dissect what happened alone. Worst—and also more likely—case? My stupid feet would find some invisible object to trip on, and I'd fall flat on my face, giving a second performance to the horde of people around us. Guess I'd go with option three: staying here and making the word things come out of the mouth hole.

"Fine," I huffed, breaking down. "It was supposed to be a joke, and then out of nowhere it wasn't freaking funny at all," I said. "Then the lights went off and he kissed me back. And oh my God, Evie, it was everything."

Her face softened as she listened. "Did he say anything afterward? Did you? Is it going to happen again?"

"No," I whispered, shaking my head. I'd burned that bridge before I even had the chance to cross it.

"When the lights came on, he looked like he wanted to stuff me in a box and mail me to a remote island. I think I really pissed him off."

"It didn't look like he was pissed from my angle, love.

The body language between you two was making *me* squirm in my seat," she said, smiling over my shoulder at Garrett as he headed back in our direction with their coats draped over his arm. "Look, if you really think you upset him, then you know what you need to do. Go find him and explain. Apologize. Bribe him with alcohol. Offer him a lap dance. You know, the stuff that usually works when you need to say sorry to me."

She turned and twerked against me, and I laughed before thanking them both for coming as Garrett helped her into her coat. Giving Evie a quick peck on the cheek, we said our goodbyes and I made my way through the crowd in search of Bash.

Thirty

MAYBE BASH HAD ALREADY LEFT. I CIRCLED THE room twice, weaving through small groups and thanking those who complimented me on my performance. I tried to keep the small talk to a minimum, because all I cared about right now was finding him and making things right. Just as I was about to give up, I felt him in the room. Even when he hated me, the connection between us remained. I swiveled around and found him almost immediately, laughing and conversing at a café table with two men. My heart fell when his eyes found mine, his smile falling. The men turned around in their seats to see what he was staring at, grinning wider when they saw me. I awkwardly lifted my hand and waved, moving my feet quickly as they both motioned for me to come over.

As I approached, the older men stood to greet me. I studied them both, equally good-looking but complete opposites. I choked back a laugh when the one with the thick, white hair slapped Bash on the back, causing him to jump out of his seat as well. Someone forgot his manners.

"Son, are you going to introduce us to your lovely costar?"

Bash did that thing where he looked past me instead of at me. "This is Callie," he mumbled. "I've, uh, mentioned her a few times."

He had? I wonder if he was warning them of my awkwardness.

The man with the white hair turned to me, blue-gray eyes crinkled at the edges like he'd lived a full life of mischief. He was about five foot ten, lean, and if it weren't for the white hair, he could've passed for early forties. His style was clean and casual, a white dress shirt tucked nicely under a brown crewneck sweater that went perfectly with his dark jeans.

"Callie, you were absolutely breathtaking on that stage, my dear. I'm in awe," he said, reaching out a hand. "I'm Max, and this is my husband, Nicholas."

"It's so nice to meet you both, and thank you, really, for the compliment. I couldn't have been Quinn without Bash by my side as Aiden," I replied, sitting in the wrought iron chair that Max held open for me.

"He's got the looks for the stage, that's for sure. But you, my darling, are stunning. Isn't she stunning, honey?" Nicholas' deep voice was so similar to Bash's. Now that I got a good look at him, he looked like Bash, just twenty years in the future. His dark black hair was thick with a slight wave, cut just above his shoulders. His frame was long and wide, comfortably filling out the black sports coat he wore over a dark purple shirt. The only thing that wasn't a carbon copy between the two were Nicholas' eyes, which were so dark brown they were almost black.

Max leaned forward, taking a sip of coffee from the Styrofoam cup in front of him. "I would've tried to snatch her up back in the day, that's for sure."

"You couldn't have gotten her even if you liked women, honey."

Max brushed off Nicholas, and I reveled in the playfulness of their relationship. I saw where Bash got it from. "So, Sebastian tells us that you two have been friends for years. After his time in England, I'm happy he had someone besides Tucker to come home to."

I looked over at Bash, who was focused on the latticework of the wrought iron table. He traced the pattern over and over, his tense shoulders making it obvious that he was uncomfortable with me being here.

"Yes, Tucker's a handful. It's like Bash and I are raising a little toddler," I said and they laughed in agreement. "We met at the beginning of freshman year." I smiled, telling them the cliffs notes version of our relationship.

We went back and forth making small talk for a few minutes, Max asking about my family and Nicholas chiming in with some cute—embarrassing—stories from when Bash was young. He stayed silent most of the time, answering with a yes or no when his parents prompted him to respond.

But not once did he look at me. I was screwed.

"You guys raised a pretty awesome human. He's been a really great friend to me. I don't know what I'd do without him." I enunciated that last part, my voice cheating in his direction, hoping he was picking up what I was putting down. I really didn't want him to be mad at me. It was making my heart ache, really freaking physically ache in my chest.

I watched as Nicholas and Max exchanged a quizzical glance and my cheeks flushed. Yeah, I had the subtlety of a wrecking ball. *Sorry, guys, you just met the queen of awkward.* I stood abruptly, aware if I stayed and talked any longer, I'd end up humiliating myself.

Unfortunately, I moved too quickly and knocked my chair over in the process, the crash echoing through the room and turning the heads of those still milling about.

Bash whipped his head around, finding me on the floor. "Did you just fall?"

"No, I got in a fight with the floor, Captain Obvious," I smarmed, rubbing my hip. "Help me up?"

Once I was standing, I shuffled around and righted the poor piece of furniture before wiping my hands on my leggings. "That chair had it coming."

Bash sat again, but this time with a smirk on his face.

Okay, fighting with furniture is an icebreaker. Good sign.

"As much as I'd love to stay and chat, I need to head

back downstairs and take all of *this* off," I told his dads, gesturing to my makeup and hair.

Nicholas moved around the table to hug me goodbye, speaking to his son and husband over my shoulder. "I hate to see you go so soon. I must admit, though, it'd be bad parenting if I let you stay. You could sneeze and overthrow the poor table, and then where would we put our coffee?"

Seriously. Older versions of Bash.

Max guffawed, slapping his hand on his knee as I stuck out my lip in mock horror. "Aw, sweetie, don't be offended. We tease because we like you," he said, wrapping an arm around me. "Does Sebastian not give you a hard time? I thought we raised him right."

"Oh, he gives me a hard time, all right," I responded. Except my brain didn't evaluate the words coming out of my mouth before I spoke, and familiar embarrassment filled my stomach. "Oh my God, no, that's n-not what—I didn't mean—" I stuttered, huffing out a breath as I picked up my bouquet of daisies.

I was going to die, right here in the lobby. That'd be fine.

Bash got out of his seat, taking the few paces between us quickly to stand next to me. Of course he was coming to my rescue again, from myself and my word-vomit. I turned to look at him, studying the complexities of his face. How could he look annoyed and jovial at the same time?

"Annnnnd that's the parental portion of the

evening," he said, ushering them away with a smile.

"Agreed. It was nice to meet you both."

As I listened to their heartfelt farewell, I backed away slowly, not wanting to interrupt their moment. When I caught Max's eye, I waved once more before heading down to the dressing room.

Thirty-One

ABOUT THIRTY MINUTES AND FIVE THOUSAND makeup wipes later, my face was clean and I'd managed to comb out the rat's nest caused by the gallon of hairspray in my updo. I threaded my hair into a loose fishtail and threw it over my shoulder. Moving to my cubby, I finagled my makeup kit into the crowded space before pulling out my crossbody bag and slinging it over my chest. Fishing my keys from the bottom, I twirled them around my finger as I turned to do a final once-over to make sure all of my costumes and accessories were back in place for tomorrow's show. If they weren't, Melissa would have my ass. Satisfied, I flipped the switch and closed the door since I was the last one there. My phone pinged. Pulling it out of the zippered pocket as I climbed the stairs, I saw that it was Tuck.

Tucker: WHERE ARE U, WOMAN? WE R HAVING FUN WITHOUT U, BIOTCH!

Callie: What do you mean, where am I? I just finished changing and stuff. I'm still at school.

Tucker: COME TO THE CAST PARTY. RIGHT MEOW.

Tucker: Or I'm going to drink all of the good booze and leave you with Smirnoff Ice.

I looked at the time—I hadn't realized it was already so late. Moving quickly through the empty lobby, I pushed through the doors and made it to my car in record time.

Callie: Tone it down, Spunktrumpet! I'll be there soon. Did you text Evie?

Tucker: She's already here. She's also guzzling the good booze with Manly McBartender.

Getting into the driver's seat, I started the car and blasted the heat. One look in the tiny lighted mirror on the inside of the visor made it apparent that I needed a quick makeover. My clothes were fine—I looked down at my hint of cleavage covered mostly by an off-the-shoulder, champagne-colored sweater. I'd loosely tucked the front into the waistband of my skinny jeans, and was thankful I'd thought to put on cute wedge booties this afternoon.

I thought I'd have enough time to go home before the party, so now I was worried about showing up half-cute. Especially since Bash would most likely be there.

It'd be much easier to play on his sympathy with my 'sad puppy' face if I had extra-long lashes and cat eyes to make my eyes bigger and shinier.

Popping the button on the glove compartment, I felt around in the dark until I found what I wanted and pulled it out. My trusty emergency makeup bag, a gift from Evie with the words "Face Shit" in dark black letters printed on the canvas.

I hurriedly swiped on dark navy eyeliner, the winged edges causing the green and yellow flecks in my eyes to pop. Pushing the little tube in and out of the mascara, I coated my lashes thoroughly before going for my concealer, using my finger to blend it into any blemishes I could find. After a quick brush of bronzer on my cheekbones and a little lip gloss, I sat back to take in the full effect. Damn, that tiny visor-light at night was like one of those ring things that beauty bloggers used.

Good job, Chevrolet.

Before I pulled out of the parking lot, I sent a quick message to Evie.

Callie: Is he there?

Evie: Oh, he's here. If he continues to drink all the vodka he can get his hands on, he's going to wake up with a Russian accent. You were supposed to find him and say sorry. Why don't you listen to me, woman? I'm the relationship guru now.

Yes, this month of having a boyfriend has made you Dr. Love.

Callie: I didn't have the chance. I'm on my way now, see you soon <3

I put the car in drive, ignoring her response until I

parked. The party was in the same apartment complex as mine, and I was thankful I could imbibe tonight without worrying about getting an Uber.

> **Evie: Btw, love...I hate to tell you this, but Bash brought a date. He's pretty cute, too.**

My stomach dropped at that piece of information. As much as I appreciated Evie giving me the heads-up, I wasn't prepared for a date. My plans included groveling and joking to get Bash and I back on good terms, not putting on a show while he was all over some guy.

I approached the apartment building, voices and music guiding me to the correct door. No one would hear me knocking over the noise, so I pushed down the latch. The door opened and I was met by friends, scattered in clusters throughout the main living area and kitchen, red cups in hand.

"Gang's all here!" Tucker shouted, pushing himself off the arm of the crowded couch. "Finally! You ready for some libations?"

Nodding, Tucker moved into the kitchen to find me something, anything, to take the edge off. Scanning the room, it seemed that almost everyone from the cast and crew were in attendance. Opening night had always been our choice for cast parties, since the next performance wasn't until twenty-four hours later. Plenty of time to recover if needed.

We'd all heard the stories from years ago, when they held them on Saturday nights. Everyone would get smashed and half the cast too sick to perform in the Sunday matinee. Rumor was, the old head of the theatre department tried to cancel cast parties altogether, but since they weren't school sanctioned, he couldn't do anything about it. Thankfully, someone decided to move it, and now we could have hangovers in peace.

Two props-department girls vacated the cramped couch and I made a beeline for the empty spot. I sank into the worn cushion, adjusting my posture before I fell deeper.

Bash came stumbling into the room from the hallway, one arm draped over a guy with a mop of copper-colored hair.

"Babe, I love you," he slurred, reaching for the wall and missing.

I watched in slow motion as he went down, his knees hitting the carpet before his face had the chance.

Fuck. My. Heart.

Babe. I love you.

Well, I guess this was the mystery boyfriend I'd been worrying about all year. I can't believe he had the nerve to bring his boyfriend to *our* cast party. Twisting the knife further, unshed tears pooled at the corners of my eyes as his date helped him up and to the couch—right fucking next to me.

"Stay," he said, holding his palm up in front of Bash's face. "I'm going to get you some water and aspirin. We need to sober your ass up a bit before heading home. No way are you puking in the Jeep."

I stiffened. Bash brushed his arm against mine as he settled, letting out a deep breath and lolling his head before his focus found my face.

"Oh, it's *you*," he garbled, lifting his index finger to my face before tapping me on the nose. "Boop." His breath reeked of alcohol, and he was being obnoxious. Why the hell was he so trashed? And how did his boyfriend and Tucker let him get this far? He stood up, struggling to maintain balance.

"Jesus, Bash. Sit back down, you're a freaking mess," I explained, guiding him next to me.

He scrubbed his face, mumbling something that sounded a hell of a lot like "it's all your fault," under his breath before yelling for Tucker.

"TUCK! Tell Callie why I'm so wasted," he shouted.

Tucker rushed over with my drink, shoving it into my hands before kneeling in front of Bash. "Brother, I love you, but you need to stop. Leave it alone tonight. Don't do this here."

I put my hand on Tucker's shoulder, crouching down when he diverted his attention to me.

"He said it was my fault, Tuck. What's my fault?"

Before he could answer, the ginger barreled back into the *wonderful* scene we'd made, a bottle water in hand.

"Open wide," he demanded, popping two pills into Bash's mouth before unscrewing the cap and handing it over.

"That's what he said." Tucker laughed.

My dirty look shut him up right quick. I was breaking, and not at all in the mood for jokes.

Bash groaned in front of us, using his arms to push off the couch again.

"SHOTS! Let's do some shots," he yelled, his arm going over his head and pointing to the fifth of vodka on the counter.

"You don't need any more. You've had enough," I scolded, following behind him.

His date and Tuck stayed behind, whispering to one another as I took care of *their* friend. It was obvious he wasn't mine anymore.

He poured way more than a shot's worth of booze into a plastic cup and brought it to his lips, his Adam's apple bobbing as he took a swig. "You know what, Callie—I *have* had enough. Enough of this back and forth bullshit, enough of having to be around you twenty-four-fucking-seven. It's torture."

Alcohol sloshed from the cup as he spread his arms wide, coating the sleeve of his thermal and spilling onto the floor. He charged into my space. His vodka-laced breath brushed my ear while he gritted out words I knew were coming. "Nothing's ever going to fucking change, Callie," he said with malice. "It's about time we get the hell over it."

Evie materialized behind me, pulling me backward as Garrett stepped in between Bash and me. Tucker and the boyfriend stood behind their drunken idiot at the ready for whatever was about to go down.

God, this whole party had turned into *West Side Story*.

Everyone in the room actually *made room* to witness the shit-show that was going on. Freaking theatre majors.

"You need to back up, man."

Bash squinted at Garrett, his head tilting slightly to the side with glassy eyes.

"Hey, you're not Callie." He laughed, turning to Tucker and whispering. "There's hair on his face. Callie doesn't have hair on her face. Right, Tucker?"

Tucker's jaw dropped as Bash mumbled something else about hair before pointing a finger inches from Garrett's face. I put a mental bonus point on Garrett's good-guy list for being so patient. If I were him, I would've already thrown a punch.

"That's—that's not who I was talking to. Where'd she go? I wasn't done talkin' to her."

Thirty-Two

"NO, HE'S RIGHT," I SAID TO EVIE. "HE'S RIGHT. I'M pathetic, and I need to stop."

Grabbing my coat from the pile in the corner, I quickly zipped and fished my keys from my pocket. It was time to go.

"He's drunk, love. No one is right when they're drunk," Evie tried.

I wish she wasn't so damn supportive, not right now, when all I wanted to do was get the hell out of here and away from Bash.

"Well, you know what they say—drunk words are sober thoughts. He wants nothing to do with me or my *bullshit*."

And then it hit me.

Bash had known about my infatuation with him this *entire* time. He strung me along on purpose.

He was a narcissist, enjoying the attention until my entertainment wasn't enough anymore. He and his *babe* probably sat at home and laughed about my pathetic crush—planning out the best scenarios to humiliate me before he'd lay the final blow and end it once and for all. Rage coursed through my veins as I changed my mind, downing the drink I set on the coffee table.

Stomping over to him, I yanked him hard by the sleeve.

"Out-fucking-side, Sebastian," I yelled, throwing a dirty look toward Tucker, warning him not to question me. "Now."

Holding the balcony door open, I stared vacantly at the wall as minutes passed, Bash stumbling his way across the room. Once he crossed the threshold, I pulled the string and closed the blinds before slamming the door shut. I was going to say my piece, and the cast, crew, our friends, his stupid boyfriend...none of them needed to see it. Feeling the wall outside the door, my hand knocked a switch and flipped it. A small sconce bathed the porch in a soft orange glow, the bulb still warming in the cold air.

"Why do you have angry face?" He tapped my nose, and if I were tall enough, I would have punched him square in the face for it. "You're cute when you're angry."

"Oh yeah? Then I'm about to be freaking gorgeous."

His brow furrowed as he backed up, his body bumping into the metal railing. "You're already gorgeous," he whispered, his hooded eyes flicking between me and the floor.

I shoved my hands into my coat pockets, the cold air a contrast against my burning anger.

"And you're sweet, and fun, and—"

His compliments meant nothing—just empty words.

"No. Just shut up, Sebastian!" I shouted. "It's my turn to talk." I paced the small distance between one corner of the balcony to the other, considering my words.

"You're a user, doing whatever you can to make yourself feel good about yourself. I enabled it for a long time," I said, laughing at my own stupidity. "And you know what? I'm better than that. I got so far down the rabbit hole that I didn't see how much I lost of myself in the process."

I looked him square in the eyes, ready to rip off the Band-Aid.

"I don't need to scratch and claw my way back out of the damn rabbit hole, Bash, because this time, I'm jumping the fuck out."

He opened his mouth to speak, and I covered his mouth with my hand.

"Don't bother. You screwed up, I screwed up, everything is messy, and I *can't* care anymore. Let's just finish the play and be done with each other."

I stomped back inside, leaving him and my heart in the cold.

An hour and a half and five drinks later, I was still at the party, still stewing in my own anger.

"We're going to head out. You should, too. Want us to walk you back?" Evie asked, hand in hand with Garrett.

I chugged the rest of my drink down to the ice. My buzz was strong after the last Long Island Iced Tea. "I'm good, you guys go home. It's only a few buildings over."

Evie was wracked with worry. I could see it in her face. I rolled my eyes at her. I was a grown up, dammit. I could handle myself.

"Seriously, go—I'm fine," I said, shooing her. She pulled her phone from her purse and flicked a switch on the side.

"I took it off silent, just in case you need me tonight." She glanced toward the kitchen, where Bash had his head in his hands, Tucker and his boyfriend flanking either side. "He can hardly think straight, love. But from what I overheard, even this smashed, all he's thinking about is you."

I watched her go, and in hindsight I should've taken her up on the offer to go home. I couldn't go home alone, not now anyway. Too much buzz for too little body.

A few more drinks would make my brain hazy. Maybe then I could fall asleep tonight.

Getting up from the couch so quickly was probably not the smartest idea. I stumbled on the leg of the coffee table, and instead of pitching to the floor, I regained some semblance of how to work my own body, which resulted in a half jog across the room. Right into boyfriend's back.

"Sorry, so sorry," I mumbled, looking at Tucker to convey the message.

Boyfriend turned around.

"It's cool, Callie. It's not the first time a chick has tried to cop a feel," he said, holding out his hand. "I know we didn't have the chance to meet earlier, but I'm a friend of Bash's. I'm—"

I don't remember giving anyone permission to tell this guy my name.

Bash turned his head just a fraction, just enough to see our interaction. He totally wanted me to play nice, see if I approved of his ginger-gentleman.

Not happening. He could take my lack of approval and shove it up his ass.

I seethed at him and held up my hand, effectively cutting him off. "Yeah, I know. *Super* nice to meet you," I snapped. I wasn't a bitch, but I wasn't in the mood to play nice. I shoved past him to the counter, grabbing the fifth of rum and refilling my drink. "I'm going to take this one to go," I said loudly, to whomever wanted to listen.

"I'll get my coat," Tucker said. "You don't need to walk by yourself in the dark. It's not safe around here."

"What are you going to do, Tucker? Garrote my potential attacker with your suspenders?"

"Wow. What the hell, Callie? I didn't do shit to you."

Bash slammed his fist on the counter. "Fuck it, I'll take her home. She's already being a bitch to me. It'll save you from her wrath."

Speechless, I walked toward the door, already itching to turn around and apologize to Tucker. I waited in the hallway for Bash, the cold air fogging with my breath.

He pulled the door closed and started walking away. "Let's go."

I stayed two paces behind him the entire ten-minute walk back to my apartment and avoided brushing against him when I moved past to unlock the door. I was majorly buzzed and pissed off, and just wanted to sleep off this whole freaking night.

"Thanks a lot for the walk."

"I'm coming in," he announced before he walked through and unzipped his coat.

"You can't just barge in when I don't *want you here*," I screeched, following him. "I don't want anything from you!"

Bash closed the space between us, his arm going past my head and shutting the door behind me. His right arm went next to my side and slid the lock into place. Bringing his hands up to my neck, he slowly released the zipper of my jacket, tugging it down the length of my torso.

"I don't want anything from you, either. Neither of us gets what we want," he whispered, his breath smelling of vodka and something citrusy. Mine surely smelled like rum, intermixing in the air between us, the combination heightening my buzz.

I shoved him off, pulling the rest of the zipper down and chucking my coat God-knows-where. Bash kicked off his boots before surprising me from behind and lifting me at the waist.

I pounded on his back when he threw me over his shoulder and started moving through the room. "Put me down, you asshole! I don't need you to take care of me!"

He groaned as I landed a pretty decent punch in his kidney area—I wasn't really great at anatomy, but I'm pretty sure that's where it was—and I kicked my legs for extra drama.

He used his free hand to locate the light switch in my bedroom and flicked it on before tossing me onto my bed. Before I had time to sit up, he was barricading the door with his muscular frame.

"Look, if you tell me to move or to get the hell out, then I will," he said, crossing his arms. "But I've had enough of your shit, Calliope. Drunk or not, I'd never force you to talk to me if you didn't want to. Please, though—just fucking hear me out, and I'll do what you ask. I'll leave you alone after the show is over."

I got up, crossing my arms to match his.

I need a drink. Get a drink, get rid of Bash, get laid.

Preferably in that order.

Preferably all tonight.

The clock said it was only midnight—I could get this conversation over with and still have time to find someone in my phone to booty text—even Tinder Jordan, if I was feeling extra desperate.

"Jesus. Fine, but I'm getting something to drink first. Get out of my way." I shoved past, walking back out to the kitchen to grab the rum from the fridge—one perk of Evie being at Garrett's all the time was that the liquor stayed where I left it—and poured one for him, one for me. I chugged mine to quell the anger that was once again rising.

"Speak," I demanded, sitting on the opposite end of the couch as him. "I don't know what else there is to say between us. You said it tonight. It's all my fault."

"I said the reason I was getting trashed was your fault, and it was, Callie."

I slammed the empty glass on the table and stood up. I didn't need this shit. "Great. *Awesome* talk. See you at the show tomorrow."

"I was drinking because I can't get you out of my head! For fuck's sake, will you stop being so goddamn stubborn and let me speak?"

I stopped in my tracks but refused to turn and face him.

"You have me all mixed up, Callie. I think about you before I fall asleep. I walk into every room and immediately look around to check if you're there.

Maybe you won't get out of my head because you mean the most to me in the entire world and you don't even fucking see it. You're my best friend—but you're so much *more*."

My heart fell into my stomach. I was so, so angry at him still, but every word dripped with sincerity. My skin heated.

I should have just fucked my attraction for you out of my system, I thought.

He turned me around and lifted my chin with his fingers.

"What did you just say?"

"I said that out loud?" I faltered. *Shit.* Tension corded in his neck as I tried to think of an explanation. Every thought came to a halt when his thumb brushed along my jaw. His lips skimmed my neck gently before he whispered into my ear.

"Yes," he said, tugging it between his teeth and sucking gently.

Tingles fired in the wake of his kisses, pure adrenaline rushing to my core.

Did he mean what I think he meant? He was buzzed—we both were.

Neither of us would remember tomorrow.

Like I could forget.

But it was Bash, after all. My best friend. Maybe having sex with him could fix all the broken parts between us. Maybe it'd stifle whatever chemistry I thought we'd have. Maybe he wouldn't even be able to get it up.

At least then I'd know for sure.

He moved from my ear and placed his forehead to mine. Strands of hair fell over my face as I looked him in the eyes. "Yes, I said it out loud? Or...y-yes, something else?"

"Yes, you can fuck me out of your system," he said deeply, tucking the tendrils behind my ear. "So let's try that kiss again."

Thirty-Three

TENTATIVELY, MY HANDS MOVED, GRASPING THE soft fabric of his shirt. I pulled him close, our bodies touching, and I was burned by the contact.

We moved backward until the hardness of the wall was flat against my shoulders. Sucking gently, I took his lower lip between my own. He groaned, and it was so fucking hot. Warm hands trailed down from my back and straight to my ass as Bash lifted me and wrapped my legs around him. I could feel the bulge in his jeans grinding against my center, and if it were possible to spontaneously disrobe from horniness, I'd be naked as fuck right now.

Fingers dug into my skin as we moved into my room and Bash turned off the light with his elbow. Soft, glowing moonlight danced through the half-open curtains, bathing my bed in a dim haze. He lowered us, and I needed to think of something other than the fact I was about to see Bash naked. I was about to have *sex* with *Sebastian.*

Holy shit.

I wrapped my arms around his neck, twining the strands of hair at the nape. I tugged gently, coaxing him close until he was fully against me and his jean-clad hips rocked into my core.

I needed to think of something distracting or I'd be the one with the embarrassing ten-second orgasm story tomorrow.

His tongue was tracing circles on my collarbone, nipping and sucking as he lowered his head.

Pineapple on pizza. Old men with hairy backs.

Bash's P is so close to my V.

My sweater and lace bralette had disappeared, and his mouth was back on my skin.

Pee-Wee Herman. Hairless cats.

Oh my God, that feels so good.

I moved my hands to the hem of his shirt and pulled up as far as I could, the fabric bunching under his chin. He sat up and pulled it off from the back of his head, just like I'd seen in movies—the way only boys could. His smirk was unwavering as he devoured my body up and down.

A shiver ran down my spine at the appraisal. I was so screwed.

Dentures. Baseball.

Bash wearing nothing but baseball pants—fuck.

He traced his index finger on the waistband of my jeans, goose bumps following his trail along my sensitive skin. He slipped the button through the hole and slowly brought my zipper down, exposing my black lace panties. "Is this okay?" he asked.

"Please don't stop," I begged, wriggling under his weight as his smile curved to the left side of his face.

God, he's beautiful.

He leaned closer, his face near my center. Never breaking eye contact, he slowly slid the soft denim down my legs before kissing my calves. Chest heaving, I lifted onto my elbows so I could soak in the sight before me. Bash's head was down and focused as he removed his jeans. Before I knew it was happening, I was at the edge of the bed, my fingers reaching out and tracing the ridges in his abdomen. That damn side-smile was back, his eyes crinkling at the edges as he watched me.

He stopped me from my perusal, covering my hand with his own. "You're breathtaking, Callie," he whispered. Lifting me gently, he touched his lips between my breasts and lowered me to the bed. His hands branded my body, setting it ablaze until he hit the thin fabric of my boyshorts. I shuddered, his deft fingers pulling them lower and the cool air hitting my heated skin.

I'm so glad I got that wax, I thought.

"I'm not mad about it," he said.

I really need to stop thinking out loud.

Alarm clocks were made by the devil. With a newfound promise to set it on fire when I was more awake, I rolled over and smashed my fist on the large button, shutting it up. My head was pounding, and I needed water to quench the desert that'd taken up residence in my mouth. Maybe some Tylenol, too— but not for the headache. Oh no, for the soreness—the delicious, aching, just-had-amazing-sex soreness.

Fuck. That totally wasn't a dream.

Slapping my palm against my face, I rolled over and saw that Bash's jeans were still in a crumpled pile on the floor. Slipping on my glasses, I got up and threw on the closest clean pair of sweatpants I could find. I grabbed a shirt from my drawer which read *'Surely not everyone was kung fu fighting'* and I couldn't even bring myself to smile as I padded down the hall.

It wasn't easy to sort through the hazy memories of last night when my brain was acting like it had been taken over by a marching band. I grabbed a few pain pills and a bottle of water and chugged, the coolness soothing the ache in my throat. Coffee was pouring slowly into the carafe and I zoned in on the drips, the sound and smell calming my nervous stomach.

Did he regret what happened? Maybe the plan to fuck him out of my system had backfired, because I was more confused than ever. He definitely had gotten it up. If I remember correctly, he'd gotten it *way* up.

Needing something to do with my hands, I loaded the dishwasher and swept the floor, keeping busy. When the kitchen was as clean as I could get it, I started folding a pile of laundry that had been sitting in the corner of the living room for days. After I finished, I picked up the pile and headed toward my room.

A quick flash of dark hair crossed my peripheral vision and panic rose in my gut. There were mere moments in which I could figure out what to say to him. I'd heard plenty of morning-after stories from Evie in the past, but they were all one-night stands with strangers. My one-night stand was with my best friend. What kind of greeting would break the ice?

Hey, so, good talk. Let's resolve all future fights that way.

Here, have some coffee. I like your man-parts.

Good morning, thanks for not putting it in my butt.

I inwardly groaned. Nothing I said would ease the awkwardness. I just needed to get it out. We had a few hours before we had to be at the auditorium to get ready for tonight's performance, and I needed a shower and a nap.

"Morning, Sweets," Bash said as he entered the room, kissing my cheek sweetly as he passed.

Uh...okay.

He raked his hand through his hair and tilted his head before nodding toward the bottle of pills. "Mind if I grab a couple of these?"

I held them out robotically, my nerves in overdrive, words begging to escape my lips. He swallowed the pills dry and I grimaced as his throat bobbed as they went down.

"So," he began, moving toward me.

Defcon two. Panic time.

I darted around him and grabbed his boots and jacket from near the doorway.

"So, uh—here's these," I blurted as I handed his belongings over.

He stared at me with an oddly hopeful expression, and that along with my headache were enough to make my brain implode.

"Thankyouforhavingsexwithme!"

He withheld his laughter before sliding his feet into his boots. "You're welcome? Sweets, that's not what I usually hear after a night of great sex."

I hid my face with my hands before throwing my arms wide. "What the hell do you want me to say, Bash?"

He reached out and motioned for me to come closer, but I remained firmly in place. Distance was safer.

"Should I have said, 'Hey, for a gay guy you're amazingly knowledgeable at giving women multiple orgasms?'"

With it out in the open, I felt a sliver of relief before his reaction happened in slow motion. All the color drained from his face as he looked at me hard, studying my expression.

"What did you just say?"

"It was a compliment, Bash," I said, shielding my face with my hair. "It's been a long time for me, and you were far better than—"

"Did you just call me gay?"

The tension from last night snapped back, surrounding us and demanding my attention. Something was wrong with the tone of his voice.

Of course I called him gay.

Why was he so offended? This was backfiring. All I'd wanted was to show my appreciation for the multiple Os he'd given me.

"I mean, you brought that guy with you last night, saying you loved him and calling him 'Babe.' I just assumed that bringing him around our friends was your way of coming out."

His skin turned an awful greenish-gray, and I worried that the gallon of vodka he'd consumed was making its way back up. I quickly grabbed a bottle of water and handed it to him.

"Gabe," he whispered after he took a sip.

"What?"

"I said Gabe, not *babe*. He's been my *best friend* since the third grade. He came up to see me perform, and I told him to make a weekend out of it," he explained. "And I said I love you because he's like a brother to me, and vodka makes me stupid."

"Oh."

Oh.

Gabe wasn't his boyfriend, he was just a friend. I replayed the events again in my head, and realized that whatever affection I thought I saw was in *my* head. Not once had they kissed, never showed any more affection than I would show Evie.

I was so stupid.

I'd completely overreacted last night, and from the look on his face, it wasn't something that would be easy to forgive.

He stood abruptly, crunching the now-empty water bottle in his fist. I stood frozen in place as I watched him slip on his coat and walk with purpose to my front door.

"You know, ever since I came back, I thought that being patient with you was the right thing to do. I thought I was doing what was best," he said, turning his head to look at me. "Just when I thought we were getting somewhere, you knock me fucking sideways."

I didn't understand what he was saying. Wringing my hands nervously, I realized it was better for me to just keep my freaking mouth shut. We couldn't fight, not now, not hours before we had to play lovers on stage again. He pulled the door open and was halfway out before turning around one last time. His eyes were hard and sad, his glare ravaging my soul.

"Oh, and in case I hadn't made it crystal fucking clear, Callie? I'm. Not. Gay."

Thirty-Four

BASH

I WAS PISSED, CONFUSED, AND THAT COMBINATION more than likely scared the shit out of the Uber driver. I practically shook the car as I closed the door. Taking the stairs two at a time, my hands shook with rage as I unlocked my apartment.

This whole time, the three years I'd known her...she thought I was *gay*?

I ripped into my room and changed into Nike shorts and a clean white tee. I needed a workout. If I didn't get some of my frustrations out before the show tonight, I'd be too distracted to perform.

The gym was almost a mile from my place. On any other day, Deftones would be coming from my earbuds and I'd jog there. Today, it was a full-on sprint, feet hitting the pavement with hard thuds, System of a Down raging in my ears.

I ran my membership card under the reader and

bypassed the locker rooms, straight to the free weights. Thoughts ran through my head as I stacked weight after weight onto each side of the bar.

The entire time I was in England, I steered clear of relationships. Sure, I brought women home, but it was never anything serious. I made it perfectly clear that it was sex, no strings.

No one came close to touching what I felt for Callie.

I slammed the bar into place and lay on the leather-covered bench beneath it. Expelling a breath, I started my reps while I sorted out the myriad of emotions going through my head.

Freshman year, my feelings for her had hit me like lightning. Callie had inserted herself into my life and there was nothing I could do to stop her. It started off small, noticing how her eyes sparkled when she laughed or the way the sun turned her hair golden. We started to hang out with each other almost daily, since Tucker and her roommate Evie were always out with some random hookup. And I loved it.

I remembered when we used to fill sandwich bags with cereal from the dining hall before taking it back to her dorm with plans for movie marathons for hours on end. Callie made me watch those vampire movies about thirty times that year—the one with the werewolves and the heroine whose facial expression never changed. She loved them. I couldn't remember a damn thing about any of those movies except the part where they explained imprinting. That's how I felt about her—like it wasn't a choice. It just *was*.

In the spring of that year, the acceptance letter for my study abroad had come and I'd never felt so divided. Wanting to explore the world while getting an education was my number one priority—before Callie. It all changed after her.

When I told her I was leaving, it wasn't hard to read the emotions written all over her face. I was gutted when she congratulated me with sincerity, completely ripped to shreds because the small smile never reached her eyes. She distanced herself after that, avoiding me to the point I couldn't even get ahold of her to say goodbye.

Once I was settled, I messaged her consistently, letting her know about my adventures and asking how she was, but all I'd get in return was a 'read' receipt. After a few months, even those little receipts stopped, and I knew she didn't want to hear from me anymore. Tucker insisted she was all right, and I practically punched the words *I'm not dating anyone* through his head—his penchant for gossip and his connection to Callie were the only slivers of hope I had to reach her.

The third set of reps were finished, and I stood to shake out my sore muscles. My breaths were still shallow, and my heart was still hurting. Wasting no time, I strode to the leg press machine and pumped the heavy weights with my legs, controlling the pace.

I thought back to the past few months. Being so close to her was torture, especially when there was nothing I could do but take baby steps to win her back.

When I left, it fractured us. I was the one who broke her trust. I was the one who left.

My dads told me time could heal all wounds, and that became my mantra with Callie. Every day, I made it a mission to make her happy without scaring her off. But the more time we spent together, the more I screwed things up. She said I'd messed with her mind, but that shit was a two-way street. Sometimes her moods changed so fast, I got whiplash.

But I stayed the course, giving her space when she asked. Yeah, I had to walk on a few eggshells to give her the time she asked for after I'd almost kissed her. Walking away from her that day was the second hardest thing I'd ever done.

Slowly, she had started to trust me again. Laugh again. She'd called *me* when she was scared that night on campus. She had texted *me* after her shitty date with Douchey McFratPants.

And then she kissed me the way she did last night, and it was all I could do not to lose it right there on the stage. And then after the cast party, watching as she came apart under me, I knew she saw the love I had for her in my eyes. I wanted her to be my forever girl. Last night was the first time in a long time I felt happy, and it was because she was in my arms.

And then this fucking morning happened and she laid the real cards on the table.

She didn't reach out to me because she felt the

same connection—she didn't even know we could *have* a connection.

Gay? She thought I was fucking *gay*.

Memories of her body against mine flooded my brain, and I winced. I didn't know what to do. Everything was wrong. Acting tonight as if I were okay was going to be the hardest performance of my life. Looking into her eyes on stage was going to be really fucking difficult. Kissing her again at the end of the show? Damn near impossible.

Sweat dripped off my skin in rivulets when I got home from the gym. The tension from this morning hadn't dissipated, even after pushing myself to my breaking point during my workout. I stomped down the hall into my room, slamming the door so hard the photos on my desk toppled over and smashed on the floor. I didn't even bother picking them up before grabbing a clean towel from my closet and trudging to the bathroom.

After a quick shower, I went into the living room where Tucker and Gabe were sitting on the couch watching TV.

"So," Gabe said, checking his watch. "How did it go? I'm assuming pretty well since you're doing the walk of shame at one p.m."

Tucker slapped Gabe's arm. "It's not the walk of

shame anymore, it's the trek of triumph. Get with the times," he retorted. "Did you and Callie kiss and make up? Bury the hatchet?"

"Oh, he buried something, all right."

If it were anyone else, I would've walked away from the heckling. Seeing as those two idiots were my best friends, they were excused. Still wanted to knock them both upside the head, though.

"Guys," I said, falling into the couch. "I told her how I felt and the look on her face—she looked like she wanted to deck me. She was so angry still, mumbled something about wanting to fuck me out of her system."

Both of their jaws dropped as they listened intently.

"I don't know, I had to make a split-second decision, so I told her 'okay.' Whatever I thought I knew about sex was replaced with this need to make her happy. It was—it was everything."

Tucker adjusted his bowtie and cleared his throat. "Oh my God. Oh my God. I knew it. All of my dreams are happening," he said, fanning himself like he was about to start crying. "What happened next? Are you together now?"

I rubbed my hands over my face and groaned. "This morning, she *thanked* me for having sex with her. Said she was surprised I was so good at giving her orgasms since I was *gay and all*."

Tucker stood abruptly and started pacing the already-thin carpet. "Excuse me? She WHAT? No offense, Sebastian, but you're straighter than a ruler."

Gabe chimed in as he peeled himself out of the recliner in the corner. "Hold up, let me get this straight," he said, rubbing his chin. "You banged, and then she told you she thinks you're gay? I've never been this confused in my life," he mumbled.

"There was no way I could reason with her, so I just fucking left."

"Probably not the best decision, brother," Tucker said, pulling out his phone. His fingers flew over the glass screen.

"You're not texting that shit to everyone, Tuck."

He turned the phone toward me for a brief moment before he continued typing. "Google has hundreds of articles about girls falling in love with their gay besties, girls falling in love with their best guy friends, but nothing on falling in love with their guy friend that they think is gay but isn't."

Gabe had gone into the kitchen to raid the refrigerator. He grabbed an apple and took a huge bite, the juice running down his chin. "Maybe you're Googling it wrong," he responded, mouth full of fruit. "Try '*how to tell the chick I love that I'm not into butt sex.*'"

"You may not be into dick, Gabe, but you are one. Stop being so insensitive. We need to help."

As I sat there listening to them argue, my mind was racing. Something needed to be figured out in the next four hours, or tonight's performance of Playing with Fire was going to go up in flames.

Thirty-Five

BASH

THE DOOR DINGED AS I EXITED THE CAMPUS store, two energy drinks in hand. I wasn't hungover, but the lack of sleep and the stress of the day had me feeling drained. After leaving the two idiots—still arguing, by the way—at the apartment, I'd figured out what my plan was.

I popped the tab on one of the cold energy drinks as I sat on a bench outside of the building. Pulling my phone from my coat pocket, I hovered over Callie's name before typing a message.

Bash: We need to talk. Can you meet me somewhere?

Callie: I don't think that's a good idea.

Her response was one I expected. She was a runner when it came to conflict, but I wasn't letting her pull that crap today. I had questions, and she had answers.

Bash: Better see if Professor James can pull an understudy out of his ass, then. If we don't talk, I don't know how I'll be able to perform tonight.

Callie: ARE YOU SERIOUS RIGHT NOW? WTF, BASH?

Bash: I think I'm coming down with something. ::cough, cough::

Callie: You're an asshole.

Bash: I try. Meet me at the Black Box in a half hour.

I switched off my phone, chugged my drink, and tossed it into the garbage. It didn't feel right to threaten the show like that, but if I had to piss Callie off in order to straighten shit out, then so be it. Nothing was going to stop me from saying my piece.

I'd been pacing back and forth across the room when Callie stomped into the Black Box in a huff. Her hair was in a giant knot on top of her head and I could see the puffiness of her eyes, her glasses unable to conceal much. She'd been crying.

I was a dick.

The need to comfort her slammed into me so hard it almost knocked me to the ground. I couldn't, though—not yet, anyway.

She shrugged out of her jacket and put her hands on her hips. "Do you want to tell me why you dragged me out of my warm bed two hours before we need to be here? Because if it's about this morning, or last night, or whether you're gay or straight, then *I don't want to talk about it*!" Tears pooled in the corners of her eyes, but it was clear they were ones of anger, not sadness.

"Well, too fucking bad, because we are *going* to talk about it. How can you be the only person on the history of this planet to be unaware of the fact that I LIKE VAGINA? My old girlfriend knew it. All the girls I banged in England knew it," I screamed at her, my hands gesturing wildly.

"Everyone knew except *you*. And how the fuck did it take you three damn years to bring it up? Maybe instead of assuming, you could've tried that crazy-shit called... wait, what is it? Oh, *asking*."

Her face had turned a bright shade of pink, and if steam really could spout out of a person's ears in anger, it would've happened at that very moment. I didn't care. I'd been riding her one-woman crazy-train long enough.

"If you thought I was gay, you could've asked one of the ten thousand students who go to this school. You could've asked Tucker. But what did you do? Absolutely nothing—you'd rather be ignorant than know the truth."

"I thought you were still in the closet or something! I was trying to be sensitive, you dick! You never dated or talked about girls. I never saw you kiss anyone. And you're a freaking theatre major, for God's sake!"

Turning away from her, I slapped my palms against the black cinderblock wall. Yeah, a lot of the guys who were in theatre in college had swung for the same team, but not me.

"So because I'm a theatre major, I'm automatically into guys? Way to stereotype, Callie. Real fucking nice."

"That's not what I—"

"Not what you meant?" I spat, pushing off the wall. "Jesus, get off your high horse."

"Get off my *ass*, Bash!" she shrieked. "Do you think it was easy for me? Knowing—no, *thinking* I was falling for my gay best friend, who also happened to be the king of mixed signals?"

She stomped over to the risers and planted herself in one of the chairs. Removing her glasses, she rubbed her eyes with her palms and sighed.

"I never said anything to you or anyone else because I was scared I'd lose you. If I didn't bring up your sexual preference, it'd be easier to convince myself I had a chance to change your mind." Her voice contradicted the words escaping her lips.

I wasn't sure how one could sound spiteful, honest, and defeated all at once, but she'd done it.

Callie rubbed her hands on her jeans and stood. I crossed my arms as she made her way to the door and picked up her coat, folding it over one arm. "This isn't going anywhere, Bash. We're stuck on this carousel of he-said-she-said and what-ifs," she remarked, her fists clenching tightly.

"So that's it? You're giving up?"

"I'm not giving up. I'm tired, Bash. Tired of this

ride. I want off. I'm exhausted, and it hurts too much. It's not supposed to hurt."

With that, she walked out the door.

Thirty-Six

CALLIE

I'D LEFT MACARTHUR IN A FRENZY, THE DESIRE to crawl back under my covers and cry a little more before the show hitting me fiercely. Knowing I needed to be back to get ready in an hour, I settled for meeting up with Evie at Chet's. *She'd know what to do.* I needed sustenance if I was going to go another ten rounds with Bash before the show.

When I got to the restaurant, Evie had clearly just arrived as she was still shrugging out of her coat. I wanted to give her a minute, let us both settle into our seats and get our drinks, but that didn't happen.

"Hey," I said, my lips twisted, full of words that needed to leak out.

"Hey?" she questioned tentatively. "Everything all right, love?"

I sat down on one side of the table and she matched the action oppositely. She was staring, waiting, and as it was with all best friends, she *totally* knew I was about to drop a bomb. Hesitantly, I opened my mouth.

"I had sex with Bash last night."

She didn't respond immediately and I took that as a cue to start my story. I stopped enough for us to order our food but not again until I was done regaling the past twelve hours.

"I know I'm the voice of reason for you—and who let *that* happen, by the way," she said and we both laughed. "I just need a moment to absorb this information." She reached across the table and held my hand. Just as she opened her mouth, the waitress returned with our food. Before speaking, Evie dipped her spoon into the bowl.

"Shit, that's hot!" Evie stuck her tongue out, fanning it with her hand. "Warn me next time!"

"Soup is hot? Sorry—soup is hot."

"Shut up and eat your grilled cheese, woman."

She blew on the spoonful of broccoli cheddar soup in front of her before tentatively placing it in her mouth. "I *still* can't believe you had sex with him."

I was about to agree with her, but she slammed the spoon down on the table and screamed.

"Oh my bloody hell, you had SEX with him! And he's *straight*!"

Heads around us turned at the volume of her voice.

"Sorry 'bout that—all is fine over here," she shouted, patting my forearm and looking around the room until we were no longer the focus.

Ugh. Is there a hole around here I can crawl into? Because that would be super.

She slouched over the table, her voice a mere whisper now. "How could we have missed that?"

I ripped off a piece of my grilled cheese, dipping it into the side of ranch before I popped it into my mouth. "You probably missed it because you weren't looking at him the way I was."

"Well, no, but I'm not naive, either. I knew *something* was off. I just can't believe we were such plonkers."

I tilted my head, confused.

"Right—idiots."

"Wow, thanks. Thank you. You're so nice." I seethed. "Remind me why we're best friends again?"

"Because every blond all-American girl needs a brunette British bird. Plus, you know that's not how I meant it. If I'd paid attention more, I would've seen the signs. He only had eyes for you, love. It all makes sense in retrospect."

She wasn't kidding. Now that I knew the truth, every single confusing moment of the past three months were made clear. I had blinders on around him, choosing only to see what I wanted to see. He was right about what he said when we argued—everything would've been easier if I'd just asked him outright.

There was always a flip side to the coin, though. We could've dated freshman year, but let's be honest—it probably would've ended the same way. He would've still gone to England and I would've still been heartbroken.

I shook my head. It didn't matter. I couldn't undo

the past.

"The only thing I can do now is move forward," I responded with fake confidence. "To moving forward without him."

"We could always reach out on Tinder again, find you someone new." She winked, tapping her glass against mine.

I'd rather chew off my own arm than go through that again. "Hard pass."

She slapped her palm on the table. "Fine. Or, you know, you could try a little harder with Bash. Why are you so willing to throw it away? You fell for him and held onto those feelings for bloody *years*. And now you have a chance, a real chance with the guy you want, but you're so stubborn and scared that you'd rather let him go than fight for it!"

Her face was flushed and her chest was heaving, and I wanted to cry at her outburst. I'd always appreciated her bluntness, but what she'd said was a little too real.

"Not all of us are lucky enough to find the perfect guy in a matter of minutes at a bar!" She recoiled, visibly upset at my attack. I was an asshole to take my frustrations out on her.

"I'm sorry, Evie. I didn't mean it like that."

"I know. And you're not wrong—I did fall in love in minutes. I want that for you, too. You deserve it, and it just seems like you finding out Bash is straight the same day you had sex was like fate. You shouldn't give up yet."

Bashful

We finished our food in silence, both of us aware that the tone was too serious for daytime conversation. She let me accept the quiet with understanding, knowing I needed more time to absorb.

With a peck on my cheek, she paid both of our tabs and left Chet's, most likely on her way to meet Garrett.

It's okay, Garrett. She's a good one to keep around.

Thirty-Seven

I BROKE AWAY QUICKLY AFTER OUR STAGE KISS that night. And that's what it truly was this time—a cold, unmoving stage kiss. Bash was tight and stubborn, and I was frigid and angry. It was palpable. Once I was safely hidden in the eaves offstage, I reflected back on the shit-show that tonight had been.

To say that the show sucked would be an egregious understatement. The audience wasn't reactive, I missed a cue due to a costume-snafu—*never* trust a side-zipper, by the way—and the chemistry between Bash and me was abhorrent. That one, I wasn't surprised about. Overall, it was the worst fucking performance I'd ever had in my life, and that included the time I played Laurie in *Oklahoma!* with the flu.

It was time for curtain call, and I wanted to be anywhere but here. Sweat clung to my skin underneath the hot lights, and I was still reeling from the tightness of the kiss a few minutes prior. With the prompt from the cast already on stage, I plastered a fake grin on my face and moved with confidence toward the gap in the center that was left for Bash and me. He moved purposefully slower from the opposite side so we didn't meet at the same time.

Seriously? This was what he was going to do?

Normally, the two leads joined hands and lifted them in a dual bow—this time, I felt nothing but air. The bastard was refusing to put on a show.

Don't let him affect you, I thought, my smile fading. *Crap. Don't let him affect you!*

We each gave a second—separate—bow and I stared at the curtain as it fell on our second performance. I didn't even stop to congratulate the rest of the members of the cast before stomping out to the lobby to meet my parents. Yeah, my parents had come tonight. I should've told them to come tomorrow for the matinee.

"Congrats, sweetie! Did you get my text earlier?" my mom said, enveloping me in a hug.

I broke away, confusion in my features.

"Um...no? But if you said 'good luck' instead of 'break a leg,' now I know who to blame."

"Calliope, you were great," she insisted, patting my shoulder.

Liar.

I stepped away and was immediately met with a faceful of roses, lilies, and my favorite, poppies. Not something that was easy to get in Michigan year-round, but somehow my parents always found a way to incorporate them in each bouquet they brought to a performance of mine.

My dad handed them off, hugging me as well. "It was good," he remarked, a knowing look breaching his features.

Leave it to Dad to do the dirty work, Mom.

He gave a knowing look to my mom, who was busy fixing an errant bobby pin in my hair. "Brenda, I'd actually like to take a look at the stability of that last set a little bit more. Do you mind bringing the car around?"

My mom's eyes danced between us, a knowing smile on her lips.

Bullshit. He didn't care if that damn set fell down on top of me. I knew right then what was happening—even at twenty-one, you were never too old for a Dad talk.

We moved through the groups of family and friends conversing with cast members until we reached the doors of the empty auditorium. Stopping at the first row of seats, I fell into the red velvet and closed my eyes.

"You don't care about the set, do you?"

I opened one eye just a smidge to see what my dad was doing. He had passed me by, climbing the steps another row and sitting behind me and two seats over.

"Callie, Mom and I love you very much, you know that. What you may not know is that even though you aren't a kid anymore, we can still read you like a book. What we watched tonight was not the girl"— he coughed—"*woman*, we know you can be. What happened up there?"

Shame flowed through my cheeks and I hung my head. My dad *really* didn't need to know about Bash and his straight tendencies—*or* that he had sex with his daughter and left—*or* that I'd never been so wrong about something in my life. That I regretted my mistakes.

"It's nothing," I said, picking at my cuticles. "It was a crappy day, that's all. Bash and I got into a fight this morning and it obviously affected our performance."

"Doesn't sound like 'nothing,'" his deep voice countered as he leaned forward in his seat. "Why did you fight? Were you fighting over the same boy? He *is* the one who likes other fellas, correct? Or was that Tucker?"

Déjà vu hit me at the same time the tears did.

"That's just it," I sniffled, turning around to face him. His face was long, a mixture of confusion and concern etched into the age lines. "I was wrong on so many levels, and we can't get past it."

I held back tears and waited for a response with bated breath.

My father furrowed his brow before leaning toward me, lips pursed. "Girlie, if there's one thing I'd hoped to knock into that head by now, it's that if you mess up, you do your best to fix it. Is he important to you?"

So, so important. "He is."

"Then get yourself together, make a plan, and fix it."

Sniffling, I wiped the tears from my eyes, careful to avoid too much mascara smearing. My dad's talks always cemented one thing for me, most of all—what I *thought* I needed to hear was what I already knew myself.

Thirty-Eight

WITH A FINAL WAVE, I BID MY PARENTS FAREWELL from the sidewalk in front of MacArthur and turned on my heels. I itched to get downstairs—*literally, the cake makeup had been on too long*—and back into my normal clothes. Moving swiftly past the few remaining lobby-loiterers, I hustled down the steps and into the dressing room.

I didn't even bother looking into the mirror before ripping a makeup removing wipe out of the package and swiping it over my cheeks. Rubbing harder, I focused on Melissa in the mirror as she sorted through the haphazard hangers piled high with discarded costumes.

"Doing okay over there?" I asked, pulling the wipe away from my face and looking at it with disgust. The foundation and blush had transformed the white cloth into a dull, dingy brown.

She sighed, righting the fabric and smoothing the wrinkles. "Two of my crew members bounced out after intermission and I was so annoyed that I let Jamie leave, too," she vented. "Whatever. I've finished putting everything away faster without them anyway."

After the third wipe, the oily makeup was still coming off by the crap-ton and I plopped down in frustration. "No more cake-face unless it's *actual* cake in my face," I said angrily, reaching farther down the counter for a bottle of toner and cotton balls. "Speaking of makeup, where's Tess? Why didn't she help you? FYI, helping isn't just girl friend code, it's *girlfriend* code."

In the reflection, I watched as she put a hanger on the rod with so much force that I swear I saw it bend.

"Don't even get me started with her. We were fighting down here during the show, and instead of talking through it, she cleaned up the makeup station and freaking *left*!"

I guess fights were the same in all relationships.

I felt bad; the soft-spoken Melissa I knew and loved had never sounded so agitated. It must've been one hell of a fight. Looking around the room, I found she really was practically done—with the exception for the costume and accessories I was still wearing. She was probably waiting for me to undressed so she could leave.

"I'll take care of my own stuff, Mel. Seriously. Go home," I insisted, tipping the bottle of toner upside down onto the cotton ball. She gave me a hesitant look, her squinted eyes shifting to the assigned space where my costumes belonged. *Oh, come on. I may be childish sometimes, but I know how to use a hanger.*

"Don't give me that look; you know I'm tidy. I'll take care of your fabric babies. Go figure things out with Tess."

Resigned, she picked up the last few scattered items and threw them in a linen laundry bag. Hauling it over her shoulder, she walked to the door. After requesting—and making me repeat it back to her—that I turn off the lights and lock the door before I left, she was finally on her way out.

Her footfalls echoed in the distance as I stood and retrieved my phone from the cubby area, reading through the five missed texts on the screen.

Mom: [photo attached]

Dear God. The picture staring back at me was my poor dog Zeus sitting pretty in what appeared to be—*oh, Mom, this is batshit, even for you*—a toga, chewing on a lightning bolt chew toy.

Mom: I know you won't see this before the performance, but your brother wanted to wish you an electrifying performance tonight! Get it?

Her mythology obsession knew no bounds. My poor dog.

Avoiding a response, I looked at the next.

Evie: How did tonight go, love? I'm at the bar, with a drink on-order for you when you get here.

My fingers flew over the keys.

Callie: You know those dreams I used to have about being naked on stage? It was that much of a nightmare.

Evie: I hope you weren't actually naked...

Callie: It may have been better if I was—maybe the crowd would have reacted slightly better if they got a view of my ass. Honestly, it was horrible. Bash and I were just so off.

Evie: Oh, love. It'll be okay. You know what? I was going to stay up here until Garrett finished his shift, but I'm coming home instead. I'll bring home cheese fries and we'll open a few bottles of vino and watch crappy reality TV.

She really didn't need to do that. She and Garrett were attached at the hip, and I didn't want to get in the way of that, even if I really needed some emotional therapy right now.

Callie: Girl, don't worry about it. I'll be fine. Enjoy your night with Garrett!

Evie: Who do you think you're talking to? LOL. I know what your I'm fine means. On my way home in five minutes, no arguing!

Ugh. No amount of convincing would keep her away.

After putting away the cleaning supplies and wiping down the counter, I slipped off my shoes and costume jewelry and stuck them into my drawer. I languidly traveled behind the screen and began to undress; Evie's 'five minutes' really meant twenty, so I could take the extra time to compose myself and unscramble my thoughts. Unzipping my skirt, I shimmied out and hung it carefully, smoothing the fabric before hanging it on a hook.

Bash and I really needed to talk again. I knew it, *felt* myself projecting it to him while we were onstage tonight. There had to be a way to apologize, to clear the air without ruining what we had before I screwed it up. All conflict aside, I loved him and I wasn't going to let him go without a fight.

Wait—did I just say I loved him?

I LOVE him. I love Bash.

I needed to get to him. Quickly, I wriggled into my jeans and pushed my feet into my boots before threading the buttons through my costume top. The blouse was over my head and I flipped it inside out to hang back up when I heard a small tap-tap-tap behind me.

"My my, Miss Miller. It seems as though I keep finding you alone."

Behind me, a voice dripped with patronization, sending shivers up my spine. I spun around, using my hoodie to cover my chest. His arm was propped on the doorframe, his knuckles relaxed after knocking on the frame. His other hand fidgeted in his pocket as his gaze traveled over my bra and stomach, slime and disgust left in its wake.

"No one but us," he said brusquely, turning his head back to the empty hallway.

"Professor James." My voice trembled. "I didn't think anyone was here."

He stepped forward, the jingling of metal in his pocket setting a sinister scene. *Oh God, not again.* He was going to touch me this time—or something worse—I felt it in my gut. Hands shaking, I moved farther behind the screen, clamoring to pull my hoodie over my bare chest.

He tsked and ambled closer. Such slow, tempered steps. He was stalking me, playing with me like I was prey. "You know, Calliope, when I recommended you practice your physical acting, it was more of a *demand* than a suggestion. You made me look inexperienced tonight in front of my colleagues." He edged forward, caging me into the corner. Panic flooded my body as I watched him lift his hand, touching my arm.

"What do you think we should do about that? A young actress as beautiful as you"—he rubbed my upper arm slowly, methodically—"should be aware they need to go to the farthest lengths to get ahead in this industry."

He winked, and any ounce of courage left in me fluttered out in waves. I wanted to scream, to shout for help, but I hadn't heard another voice since Melissa had left. Would anyone hear me?

Get away. Fight. Do something, Callie.

I remained frozen, unable to move.

"It's a shame you didn't listen to me," he spat harshly, his hand gripping me hard enough to bruise.

266

He brought his face closer to mine, sniffing along the length of my neck.

I wanted to throw up, to punch him, to do anything. *Why couldn't I move?*

"Fear not, Calliope. I'll make sure you learn the real way to get ahead."

I whimpered, tears forming. "P-please, Professor James, don't do this."

Thirty-Nine

BASH

TONIGHT SUCKED.

I'd quickly changed into my street clothes after the disaster of a performance, desperate to get the hell out of MacArthur. It was better to keep my mood away from everyone else—one wrong word and I wouldn't be capable of keeping my cool.

But as I walked through campus, a heavy knot formed in the pit of my stomach. Did Callie already leave? Did someone walk her to her car? I knew how skittish she was at night. I'd seen the terror in her eyes that night after our first Black Box rehearsal. Fighting or not, her safety was more important than my stubbornness. Her *everything* was more important than my stubbornness.

Doubling back, I hustled through the open doors and down the stairs toward her, toward my girl. She needed to know the truth—that I was falling for her. I was pretty sure I'd fallen all the way in already. As pissed as she made me, the good outweighed the bad, and the past could stay there. I would fix this.

I moved toward the girls' dressing room with purpose, fully prepared that she may not be there. Regardless, I'd find her tonight, make sure she was safe, and then kiss the shit out of her. All the words could come later, after this nagging feeling left my stomach.

That's when I heard a male voice.

And then *hers*.

I halted in front of a cinderblock entryway that led to another room, holding in my breath. Backing into the shadows and out of sight, I peered past the corner to witness him sauntering toward her and growling, "*no one but us*."

That motherfucker.

So that's who Callie was running from that night. I should've known our piece-of-shit director had no fucking boundaries. I'd witnessed the way she never spoke to him, never made eye contact with him during rehearsals. *I can't believe I didn't see it.* My blood boiled and I wanted nothing more than to march in there and beat the shit out of him—hell, I still wanted to. Mind racing, a myriad of scenarios went through my head and I knew there was only one way to get out of this without consequence. I quickly hit the button on my phone and waited.

Anger had never coursed through my veins so hard, pumping into every nook and cranny until my adrenaline caught fire. The fierce need to protect Callie, the magnitude that I was standing here was nothing compared to what I'd do if I didn't have to worry about the repercussions. As soon as I heard her whimper, the rage magnified into a ball of fire. Nothing was going to stop me, evidence or not. No way was that bastard going to hurt her. I stepped out of the shadows and into the room.

It took all of four strides to reach him, and I gripped his jacket with my fist and ripped him away from a visibly shaking Callie. Her eyes shone in fear as tears rolled down her cheeks.

"I'd ask what the hell was going on in here, but you've made it pretty fucking clear what was about to happen, you disgusting piece of shit." I shoved him out of the way and rushed to Callie, placing my hands gently on her cheeks and studying her. Her chest was heaving as she gulped for air and I brought her closer to my chest.

My thumb stroked her skin softly, wiping away a tear. I soothed her as best as I could, whispering my worry. "Hey, you're okay, you're okay, I'm here. Are you all right? Did he hurt you?"

She shook her head, silent tears soaking into my shirt.

"Sebastian—" I heard behind me, the confidence in his voice causing me to rage all over again.

I kissed Callie's forehead with the faintest trace of my lips before I turned, stalking toward Professor James. With force, I slammed my palm into his shoulder and backed him up against the wall.

"You *assaulted* her. You *harassed* her. I'm reporting you, asshole. There's no way you're getting away with this," I spat through clenched teeth.

"Take your hands off me, son, or you're never going to step onto this campus again. I'll make sure of it." He seethed.

I released him, crossing my arms and blocking the doorframe in case he tried to leave. Callie was still behind the screen, peering anxiously at me as Professor James stood straighter and put his hands in his pockets, an icy smile growing on his face.

"Assault is a very serious accusation, Sebastian. One I've had claimed against me in the past, as a matter of fact. The funny thing about that"—he squinted, and a hateful chuckle escaped his throat—"is that I'm still here. That student's claim was thrown out and she left in the middle of the semester without any of it marring my name."

"You see, the thing about being a theatre professor in a position like mine is that I know a *lot* of people, and my acting experience can convince just about anyone of anything," he snarled. "Your word—and Miss Miller's word—against my own? Sorry, son. It'd fall on deaf ears. I wouldn't suggest that."

If he called me son one more time, I'd knock him out. He didn't deserve to call anyone that.

His eyes flew to my hand, clenched and ready to strike. "Now a student assaulting a professor? That would have serious ramifications. I'd suggest you two walk away from this and never speak of it again. You wouldn't want to lose your credibility so close to graduation."

His words were a verbal blow straight to my head. The worst part about assault was what happened when the victims were silenced, made to feel guilty about something that was never their fault. Callie didn't deserve that, and I felt awful for the girl he'd done this to in the past. I couldn't—wouldn't—let him get away with this again. I'd rather lose my degree and risk a potential investigation than let him think he was walking out of here without repercussions.

"Walking away is not going to happen."

Lifting my fist from my waist, I prepared for the worst when Callie rushed across the room. She clasped her hands around mine, her once-fearful eyes now alive with fire and frenzy.

"Let me do this, Bash. I need to do this," she whispered, reaching around my waist to wrap her arms around me in a quick hug.

I watched her intensely, remaining close enough behind her that if she needed backup, I'd be there. She stomped toward him, her frame tense and worked up. "What you've done is a direct reflection on the kind of person you are, *Professor*," she spat. "I'm not going to let you do this to me or another girl *EVER again! We deserve better!*"

Pride burst through me when Callie found her

voice. *There's my girl.* That pride grew to exponential heights when I watched her lift her boot swiftly and kick Professor James straight in the junk—hard.

Forty

CALLIE

I WATCHED AS THE RAPEY-BASTARD'S KNEES buckled and he went down in a collapse of limbs and groans.

"I'm going to tell everyone on this campus who you really are. Believe me, I won't stop until the dean, your colleagues, and every student I've ever met know about the professor who disrespects and takes advantage of his students," I seethed, my chest heaving. I jerked slightly when sinewy arms wrapped around my frame, relaxing instantly when I realized it was the only other person in the room. Someone who wouldn't hurt me. Someone who always made me feel safe.

Home.

"Oh, and, James?" Bash spoke, pulling his phone from his pocket. "I recorded it—*all* of it, from the minute you started harassing Callie." He dangled the phone in front of him, the recording clearly visible on the screen. "Whatever leg you thought you had to stand on is gone now. You're done."

I love him.

He was going to throw his education out the window to protect me, even though he had evidence in his pocket. He would've done that—for me. It took everything in me not to kiss him at the exact moment.

"Since you're so fond of suggestions and demands, Professor, I highly *suggest* you don't show up to the performance tomorrow. I'll make sure security is there just in case."

He groaned, rolling on the floor with his hands still cupping his crotch. I squealed internally. Hopefully he'd be icing his nuts until the dean of Michigan College called him in for a statement.

"Bash?" I asked, grabbing my purse and putting my glasses on. I wanted nothing more than to be done with the professor and be alone with him. "Can you drag him into the hallway? I promised Melissa I'd lock up."

As soon as Bash removed the *trash*, he intertwined his fingers with mine and didn't let go until we reached his apartment. Still reeling from everything that went down, I turned the ignition off in a daze.

"Hey," he whispered, and I turned my head. Reaching his arm out, he tucked a small strand of hair behind my ear. "You're safe."

Even though I knew tomorrow was going to be the beginning of a very lengthy, very taxing battle, his words soothed my battered nerves. Maybe the recording wouldn't be admissible, or maybe Professor James was right when he spoke of his clout with the administration. All I knew right now was that he didn't deserve any more of my time tonight.

The person who deserved my time was sitting right next to me, patiently waiting for any semblance of a response. Blinking my thoughts away, I gave him the first genuine smile I'd felt today.

"You came back for me," I murmured, adoration in my eyes. He smiled back as I unbuckled my seatbelt and reached for the door handle. "Just sit right there, okay? It might be too soon for jokes, but we've had enough drama today. I don't need you falling when you get out. We wouldn't want to make a hospital trip on top of everything else."

"Too soon," I screamed, giggling at his attempt to lighten the mood. His built frame was on display thanks to the headlights and I admired it as he rounded the hood and opened my door. He offered his hand, helping me out of my seat before grabbing my bag and tucking it into his side.

"Come on, Sweets. Let's go inside and get warmed up—put something in you."

Giggity.

"You really need to stop thinking out loud, woman. I meant coffee, some food, maybe a shot."

"Damn it." I felt my cheeks redden. Apparently, even in the most stressful times, my inner twelve-year-old-boy came out.

After unlocking the door, Bash and I walked in to see Tucker and Gabe huddled close on the couch, covered up to the neck with throw blankets, their gazes fixed on the television.

"You're home late," Tucker droned, still glued to the TV. I'd already hung up my coat and taken my shoes off before he finally spoke again. "Where were— oh, CALLIE! I take it you two made up? What did I miss? A little nookie after the show? What about—"

I could tell that Bash was getting agitated. We hadn't even figured things out between us yet, and it wasn't going to happen if nosy-nelly stayed here. Tucker was nosy, but thankfully he was also easily distractible.

"Are you guys Netflix and chilling? You're awfully close on that couch," I implied.

Bash chimed in as he walked to the kitchen. "I'm surprised they aren't sharing one blanket between them."

"Blame Tucker! He's the one who insisted on this movie. I'm never going to be able to sleep tonight! The horror!" Gabe put both palms on his cheeks and dropped his jaw.

When I had enough of his theatrics, I turned to look at the movie they had chosen.

"Are you kidding me?" I slapped my palm to my forehead. "*Labyrinth*? You're telling me that David Bowie in a pair of spandex tights is going to give you nightmares?"

"*Any* guy in a pair of spandex tights is enough to

give me nightmares. Plus, he's always got balls in his hands," he argued, shuddering.

Bash exited the kitchen and handed me a short glass full of amber liquid.

"Why's he gotta fondle the balls? Oh God, they zoomed in on his codpiece!"

Gabe covered his eyes with his hands, opening a small slice between his fingers to peek through. Tucker lifted one eyebrow, clearly enjoying the scene unfolding next to him. "You know what a codpiece is? Are you sure you're straight?"

"And on that note," Bash intervened, picking up the remote from the side table. "Why don't you take Gabe out to the bar for a while, maybe buy him a pitcher of beer since you've scarred his manhood for life."

"It'll never leave my brain," he cried.

Such an idiot. I swirled the drink in my hand, the ice cubes chasing one another around the glass. I swallowed a sip, the strong taste of bourbon burning my tongue. I just wanted to be alone with Bash, and from what I could tell, he did too.

"Fine, fine, come on, big guy." Tucker sighed, offering his hand to Gabe.

He slapped it away. "I'm not taking your hand, you trust-killer."

I watched as they both slipped on their shoes and coats before heading out. Finally. Bash and I locked eyes, smiles of relief on both of our faces. "So."

The door reopened the tiniest amount. "Psst!"

Tucker whispered, only his face visible in the gap. "Text me if we need to find somewhere else to stay tonight, *wink wink*. Leave a proverbial sock on the door, if you know what I mean."

Bash rushed toward him, putting his hand over Tucker's face and shoving him out of the way before closing the door.

"Wait, we need a code word!"

I watched as Bash put his forehead against the door, sighing as he flicked the lock. After a garbled "he smeared my glasses," came from the other side, it was silent and I knew we were finally alone.

Forty-One

SMILING NERVOUSLY, I SWITCHED THE GLASS from hand to hand, waiting for him to turn around. It wasn't lost on me that he was probably waiting for me to make the first move, say the first thing. Mustering up all the courage I could, I whispered the second-most phrase he needed to hear. The phrase I owed him before I could say the other words.

"I'm sorry."

Bash lifted his head and turned ever so slowly, his eyes dark.

He needs to hear more than that—okay. Tell him how you feel. I chewed my lip, trying to find the words. "I'm sorry about what happened this morning, and I'm sorry for being a freaking idiot for three years, but I'm *not* sorry for last night. Even if you never want to talk to me again, I'll never forget how connected I felt"—I stumbled with my words—"feel with you."

I waited eagerly as he stayed locked in place, his

eyes hooded and jaw clenched.

Say something, anything.

He remained a few yards away from me, the silence prickling my skin. I backed away and placed my glass on the table next to the couch, avoiding eye contact, his burning gaze too painful for me to bear any longer.

"Thank you for coming back for me tonight," I mumbled with my back turned, discreetly taking off my glasses and setting them on the table. Nothing was worse than crying with glasses on, and I could see that this might be headed in that direction. *Again.* "I don't know what would have happened if you hadn't been there." I inhaled slowly, focusing on the carpet fibers.

"Callie."

My stomach fluttered at the sound my name made on his lips; he spoke it with such tender strength. I turned slowly and lifted my head a fraction, just enough to see him stride across the room and land in front of me. My chest heaved at his proximity, each heavy rise brushing against his shirt before he wrapped an arm around my waist and pulled me to him.

"I'll always come back for you."

My eyes shuttered closed, drowning in the warmth of his body wrapped around mine. I just wanted to soak there a little longer.

"Callie," he whispered, stroking his thumb along my jaw and pulling me back to the surface.

"I can't wait anymore."

He kissed me before I could respond, his lips

crashing against mine with more passion than I'd ever experienced. Our first kiss was amazing, but this one was exponentially...*more*. This kiss wasn't simple, it wasn't an everyday kiss. No, this kiss spoke to me. It screamed to the heavens that I wasn't falling for Bash—I was too late for that. I was head over heels, insta-butterflies, can't-live-without-him in love.

Bash palmed my face with both hands and tilted my head slightly, the minuscule action fusing our mouths even closer. Warmth spread from my belly to my chest like wildfire as he lowered his hands to my ass, scooping me up before they moved to the underside of my thighs, wrapping them around his waist. My hands twined in the dark hair at the nape of his neck as he kissed me feverishly, taking as much as he could give. He nibbled on my lower lip, the movement so unexpected that I inhaled sharply. The groan that came out of his mouth was *hot*.

Holy hell.

His teeth tugged at the tender flesh as I pulled away, the shock on my face apparent. Everything was so intense, so fast. I knew where this was headed and my body hummed with excitement.

"Take me to your room." I peppered kisses along his jaw, following the sharp line until I hit his ear. Taking it into my mouth, I wrapped my lips around it and sucked, tugging the lobe with my teeth and he shuddered. Goose bumps prickled his neck, and I continued the assault on the other side as he carried me down the hallway.

I was hot, wet, and full of ovary-exploding need as he put me down slowly, each inch sending me into a frenzy. When my feet were finally on the ground, he lowered his head and kissed me again, kicking the door closed with his foot at the same time. *My little multitasker.* My hands flew to his pecs, traveling down the hard planes of his abs before reaching the hem. I slipped my fingers under the soft fabric and dragged my fingernails softly along the sensitive area between his hipbones, my plans to go lower dashed when he clasped my hands in his own and lifted them away.

With shallow, heavy breaths, Bash broke away, and my heart ached at the absence of his lips on my own. I rubbed them with my fingers, feeling the swollenness and imprinting it into my memory. His expression blazed with heat as he focused on my body with hooded eyes.

"If we don't stop now," he huffed, "I don't know if I'll be able to. I want to do this the right way, Sweets. I want you to know how much you—"

I want to implode, too. Don't be a gentleman right now.

"Shh." I placed a finger over his lips. "I never said stop."

Kudos to his noble ways of wanting to do this right, but I wasn't having it. We *were* going to have sex tonight, dammit. Mustering up as much courage as I could find, I confidently gripped at the fabric on his chest and spun him, the backs of his knees hitting the edge of the bed. I promptly pushed against his stomach until he fell backward, landing on his elbows. I climbed on top of him, my legs straddling him and my core hitting the hardness in his jeans.

"Please let me take off your shirt, Bash," I asked sweetly, bunching the cotton up his abs. They contracted as I dragged the fabric farther, stopping for him to lift it over his arms and head. A little dirty teasing was fine, right? I smiled devilishly before lowering to his skin, trailing kisses down until I hit the faint hair of his happy trail. Tugging the waistband of his jeans down slightly, I sucked and nibbled at the inner hollow of his hip bone.

He bucked off the bed, grunting my name. *Yeah, I knew that was a sensitive spot.*

"Did I do something wrong?" I asked innocently, toying with his belt with a small grin on my face.

"You're evil," he moaned, scrubbing his hands over his face. "Torturous."

My grin stretched even farther across my face as I undid his belt and popped the button of his jeans through the hole.

"Bash?"

"Y-yeah."

He was breathing heavily. This game was fun.

"I'm going to take your pants off now."

Forty-Two

I LICKED MY LIPS AS SOON AS HIS BOXER-CLAD cock sprang free of his jeans. Scrambling off the bed, I removed the bunched denim before wriggling out of my own and climbing back on top of him. This sexy, confident version of myself was normally so out of character for me, but I felt completely at ease—this wasn't some random guy. This was Bash, and he was looking at me like I hung the stars.

His rough hands gripped my waist, shifting us on the bed until he lay flat. Anticipation built in my core and I couldn't help rocking slowly against his boxers, the friction shooting pleasure straight to my head. My nipples tightened as I continued to grind against his cock, warmth growing in my belly. Bash slid his palms up my thighs before he reached around and cupped my ass, lifting me just enough that when I came back down, he was grinding directly against my sensitive clit.

"Oh my God," I moaned, my hands flying to my

breasts.

I felt everything through the two scraps of fabric between us as I rubbed against him harder. He startled me, bunching the fabric of my shirt over my head in one swift move. My eyes flew shut as he cupped each breast, weighing the heaviness in his hands. I threaded my fingers behind his neck and held on for dear life, unable to control the pace of my writhing at each pass of his thumb over my nipples.

Bash growled, a shudder running the course of his body before propping up on his arms to kiss me. In no time he'd unclasped my bra and wrapped his arms around my waist, carefully flipping me so I was on my back. He tipped his head, worship in his glance as he looked me over, studying my body.

"You're so fucking perfect, Callie," he whispered, kissing a trail down from my collarbone to my breasts. He ravaged them until they were tender, the stiff peaks zapping waves of pleasure to my core.

There was no semblance of time as I fell deeper, focused on the heat building in my belly. Before I knew it, Bash was at my waist. He twisted his fingers around the waistband of my boyshorts and slid them off. I shivered as his hot breath danced up my thighs, intensity building as he teased the sides of my opening with kisses.

The tip of his tongue stroked upward until he hit my sensitive bundle of nerves. My body caught fire from the inside out as Bash's tongue stroked my clit repeatedly, every cell spontaneously combusting. Muscles I didn't know I possessed tightened as he built me up higher, the pleasure overwhelming. "Don't stop, please," I begged, climbing toward the peak. Just when I thought I couldn't any longer, he sucked my clit hard and I bucked off the bed.

Bash rode out my orgasm, his tongue flicking up and down until I was satiated. My chest heaved, begging for oxygen as I recovered.

"Oh my God," I whispered, the molten embers reigniting inside me as I got an eyeful of his hard cock.

He smirked and moved up my body and kissed me. I tasted myself as he thrust his hips into my center. I needed him inside me. I whimpered and moved my hands lower, struggling to reach his boxers. *Damn short arms.*

"Bash," I moaned. "I need...I need..."

He nuzzled into my neck and mumbled, "Whatever you want, it's yours."

My neck had always been my sweet spot, and a wave of goose bumps danced along my skin. "I can't reach your boxers," I groaned, a full shudder overtaking me as he drove into me again.

He lifted his head so we were nose-to-nose, his full-dimpled smirk on display. He let out a small laugh.

"God, I love you," he said sincerely, adoration shining in his eyes.

"Like *love me* love me?" I gulped, my eyes wide. "Or are you saying that because I blurted something awkward again? Or maybe because——"

"Callie," he said gently, but with a firmness that told me this was no joking matter. "I love you, with my whole heart. I've always loved you. I'll never stop."

Warmth flooded my veins, bursting into my heart with those three little words. "I love you too, Bash."

He kissed me tenderly, both of us ready for what was yet to come. Pushing him back ever so slightly, I grinned and propped myself up on my elbows as he slid off the bed. I watched as he quickly removed his boxers and pulled a foil packet from the drawer in his nightstand.

Watching Bash sheath himself was *hot*, and I wanted nothing more than to scramble off the bed and climb him like a tree—until he one-upped his own sexiness. I eyed him hungrily as he took his cock into his hand and almost died when he slid it between my folds.

"Don't tease me, please," I begged. I couldn't take it much longer. In one swift thrust, Bash entered me and I gasped as I felt myself stretch around his length.

With a shaky breath, Bash began to pump slowly. Another orgasm was building and I gasped, the multitude of sensations bringing me close. I wrapped my legs around him and pulled him into me harder, faster.

"St-stop," he groaned, his face pained. "If you don't slow down I'm going to come a lot quicker than I'd planned, Sweets." He closed his eyes for a second and let out a controlled breath.

I clenched my walls around his cock, the devilish look on my face all he needed before gripping my hips and returning to the speed I'd set. He tilted his head down and ran his tongue around one nipple, biting it as he pounded relentlessly. I was so close again. I'd never had two orgasms back to back—I didn't know if I could.

I experienced that fine line between pleasure and pain, my body screaming as he worked me with his length and his thumb.

"Come with me, Sweets," he begged as our rhythm increased.

I shuddered in response. I slammed my eyes shut, stars bursting behind my lids as I came. He leaned forward and crashed his lips again mine, groaning into my mouth as he pulsed inside me.

He pulled back and rolled over, bringing me with him until I was settled into the crook of his arm.

"Holy shit."

"*Holy. Shit.*"

Forty-Three

WE LAY TOGETHER UNTIL OUR BREATHS returned to a normal level, the oxygen welcome to our brains. Bash stroked the side of my stomach gently, and I relished in the sweetness. We'd waited so long to connect, and now that we had, it was like a puzzle had finally found the missing piece.

"So this didn't mean anything, right?" He kissed the top of my head.

I jerked up, squinting at him before punching him in the chest.

"You're such a dick," I smarmed.

"You enjoyed this dick, according to all those noises you made."

"Oh my God," I groaned and fell back into him.

"Hey, I proved what you said, didn't I? Pretty sure you said I was 'extremely knowledgeable at giving women orgasms.'" He smirked cockily. Such a little shit.

"Meh." I pretended to study my cuticles. "You could

use some practice."

In a flash, he was on top of me again, caging me in. "Oh yeah?" He kissed me sweetly. "We can practice again right now," he said at the same time he started to harden again.

I thrust my hips upward just as my phone pinged from somewhere in the room.

"Shit!" I scrambled off the bed, pulling the blanket around myself as I searched. Lifting my jeans from the floor, I ripped it from my back pocket.

"What's wrong?"

"It's Evie," I told him, scanning through the multiple variations of 'SOS' she'd sent to me.

"After the performance, she went back to our apartment to wait for me. I completely forgot to text her after everything that happened, and then we got here, and, well," I implied. She was probably getting ready to call the police, if she hadn't already. I scanned to her last text, sent just a minute or two ago. My thumbs flew over the screen as I punched out a response.

> Evie: If you're not lying in a ditch somewhere, I'm going to find you and kill you. TEXT ME BACK!

> Callie: I'm alive. And if you killed me, you'd have no one to do your laundry. I'm at Bash's place.

> Evie: You're WHERE?! Now I'm the one who's dead. Why are you there?

I smiled and glanced over at Bash, who was patting

the open space between his legs. Crawling back onto the bed, I settled in front of him as he wrapped his arms around me and settled his chin on my shoulder.

Before I could respond, the front door slammed and the noise echoed throughout the apartment. "Honeys, we're home!"

I jumped off the bed, frantically searching the room for my discarded clothing.

"I can't find my underwear!" I whispered to Bash in a panicked frenzy.

He lazily rolled off the bed, strolling toward me in all his glory. It wasn't until he backed me up that I spotted them in the corner. "You don't need those," he grinned before reaching around and opening a few drawers.

He handed me a black T-shirt and boxers before grabbing some for himself. After I had put them on, I caught a glimpse of myself in the mirror. The T-shirt was so big on my tiny frame you could barely see an inch of the boxers underneath. The sleeves went down to my elbows.

"I look naked," I said, crossing my arms over my chest.

Bash wrapped his arms around me from behind and stared at my reflection.

"You look beautiful," he whispered, tilting his head to kiss my cheek. Breaking away, he slapped my ass playfully before unlocking and opening his bedroom door. "For the record, you in my T-shirt doesn't even come close to how amazing you look naked." He winked. "But it's a close second."

I rolled my eyes, secretly relishing in the warmth that his compliment brought me.

"I'll be right back, Sweets. I'm going to go tell the guys to leave us alone tonight. Do you want anything from the kitchen while I'm out there?"

I was still soaking in happiness and covered from head to toe in post-sex glow. Nothing Tucker and Gabe said would faze me, and truthfully, Tucker seeing me this happy might *really* freak him out. I giggled, standing on my tiptoes to place a kiss against Bash's lips.

"I'm just going to text Evie real quick, and then I'll be out there. Maybe we can all watch the rest of *Labyrinth* together," I said, and Bash just shook his head.

"See you in a minute, then. I love you, Sweets."

So much internal screaming happening right now.

"I love you too." I beamed at him before he walked away and laughed when he turned back around and caught me staring at his ass. I went back to the bed and picked up my phone.

Evie: So help me God if you just ghosted on me again.

Evie: ......

Evie: I'm going to unfriend you everywhere in 5, 4, 3, 2....

Callie: OMG, woman! Are you sure you're not the drama major? ::face palm::

Callie: Everything is freaking perfect.

Callie: He loves me.

Evie: WHAT?!

Callie: And I love him. We're in love. It's good. REALLY good if you know what I mean.

Evie: Love, I'm so happy for you! I knew it in my heart that you were soulmates.

Evie: Also, though—'it was good'? GIVE ME DETAILS RIGHT NOW!

I scanned Bash's room absentmindedly as I tried to think up a response that would convey my need to keep our relationship close to my heart, at least for a little while. My eyes landed on his bookshelf, and I walked over to it and crouched down. Love filled my chest as I stroked the spines of the romance novels on the bottom shelf, and I realized why.

We loved each other as fiercely as the characters in those books, and I knew it with all of my heart. This kind of love was precious, and I wasn't going to let it go. Knowing my answer, I stood and typed it quickly before throwing the phone on the bed and walking away to meet my man.

Callie: Sorry, these lips are sealed. You know I'm bashful about that kind of thing. ;-)

THE END

Epilogue

BASH
FIVE YEARS LATER

"OKAY. YEAH, MAYBE FIFTEEN MINUTES OUT. I'LL be there soon."

I ended the call and slid the phone back into my pocket, continuing my walk toward the CIBC Theatre. I half-jogged across the street, weaving around those who walked too slowly. As I moved with purpose, I thought back to all of the shit Callie and I had to go through to get where we were today.

After we finished Playing with Fire, I watched in awe as Callie gracefully dealt with the aftermath of Professor James' assault. She'd shocked me more than once with her maturity and strength throughout the sordid process. Once the story leaked and hit the local news stations, a former student named Jade came forward as well and filed sexual assault charges against him. With her report, Callie's statement, and my evidence, it was more than enough for the court to charge him. It was a hard few months, but it was worth it in the end. Callie and Jade were satisfied, and our bastard of a director was behind bars.

We made it through the rest of the year by sticking close to our group of friends, focusing on finishing school and auditioning for post-grad Summer Stock theatre—together. We could get through anything as long as we had each other. When we graduated, we both landed paying gigs doing Summer Stock in Pennsylvania—her in Philly and me in Allentown. We made the short distance work, sharing an apartment between the two and spending most of our time outside of rehearsals exploring the city—and each other.

About six months ago Callie and I had arrived in Chicago, fresh-off a stint with a national touring company performing *Rent* six times a week. Seeing her face light up on stage night after night was worth every exhausting second. Don't get me wrong, I loved acting as much as she did, but living in and out of suitcases for months at a time was exhausting.

When I sat her down after the show ended, we had a long conversation about long-term goals. Mine had shifted, and I wanted to do more behind the scenes. Callie completely supported my dream of going back to school for my master's degree in Theatre Lighting Design. I'd applied to a lot of schools, but when I found the one here, it was like fate smiled down on us. The week I'd received my acceptance email, we were in Chicago on a quick getaway. Callie had fallen in love with the city and decided she was ready to put down some roots, too.

The signal at the crosswalk flashed orange and I stopped, glancing at my watch. I needed to get to the theatre and fast. Everything was planned to a T, and I'd never forgive myself if I screwed it up.

Callie had just started rehearsals for a brand-new pre-Broadway show, and it was the talk of the town. Her name had been in the news, on the theatre message boards, and I felt it in my bones that this show would be her big break. I was so fucking proud of her for making her dreams come true. Luck had been in my favor and I'd scored a job on the lighting crew for the production, and it was like everything had fallen into place. With the experience I was gaining in my new job, and everything I was learning through my master's program, I was well on my way to reaching my dreams, too.

My dads would check in constantly, begging for updates about us and the show. It didn't take long for them to love my girl as much as I did. Her parents were the same, albeit a bit weirder. I'd never want them to change, though—Callie's quirks came from them and I adored each one. Every time they called she would roll her eyes, pantomiming as her mom attempted to convince her that the Greek gods had a part to play in all of it. She'd laugh it off when her mother explained that a love like ours didn't just fall into place.

But I started to think maybe she was right.

I reached West Monroe Street and glanced up at the marquee for the CIBC. Shuddering, I pulled my phone back out and opened the group text. Everyone needed to be in place if this was going to work. Plus, we had a reservation across town to celebrate.

If she said yes.

Bash: I'm outside. What's her ETA?

Evie: Almost there – five minutes! Stop texting me, she's getting suspicious!

Brenda: We're on the balcony with your dads!

Tucker: Just got here. It took me forever to tidy up and set the romantic ambiance for later. Dude, your condom is super dirty.

Tucker: CONDOM

Tucker: CONDO. You two have a dirty CONDO. Jesus.

I rushed down the alley and into the unlocked side door that a coworker had left open for me. My hands were shaking horribly as I made my way up on stage.

Two minutes to go.

The cavernous space was dark with the exception

of the small track lights that lined the aisles. When the double doors creaked at the entrance, I heard a distant British accent followed by a slam.

With that one noise, that simple sound, the guys upstairs took their cue. An electric spotlight rotated behind me toward the doors, casting Callie in a halo of light.

She was stunning. I took in her curves, highlighted by a retro black dress that poofed out past her hips. Her hair fell in soft waves past her collarbones, and I wanted nothing more than to have her next to me.

"What's going on?"

"Walk straight toward my voice, Sweets."

"I can't see anything!"

Maybe the spotlight was a bad idea.

I could see her, but knowing she was basically blind, plus her penchant for hurting herself? She'd probably fall down the steps before I could ever get the ring even close to her finger.

Jumping off the stage, I took the steps two at a time until we met in the middle.

"Babe, seriously...what are we doing here?"

Taking her hands in mine, I glanced around the auditorium. Hundreds of folded, elegant velvet seats stared back.

"Look at all these empty chairs, Callie. Each and every one will soon be filled with people who are in awe of your talent, your beauty, and your heart."

Her face flitted down to where we were joined,

without a doubt worried about how hard I was shaking.

"I've been in awe of you since the second I met you. We've been through so much, Sweets. Some would say we've been through the performance of a lifetime."

She laughed lightly, and I knew she agreed.

"The thing is, no matter how much drama we have to deal with, I wouldn't want to do it with anyone but you. I love you more than anything. All those people in the audience can have you when you're up on that stage, but I promise I'll always be your number one fan."

Her breath hitched as I got down on one knee.

"Calliope Ann Miller, will you let me play the biggest role I'll ever have and let me be your husband?"

Silent tears streamed down her face as I pulled the velvet box from my pocket. I opened it, the sparkling two-carat vintage ring casting rainbows on her skin. "Marry me, Sweets."

In typical Callie fashion, a simple yes or no wouldn't do. She threw her arms around my neck and tackled me, both of us falling backward as she crashed her lips against mine.

"YES! So much yes," she cried.

Shouts and applause came from our family in the balcony as I kissed her beautiful face.

It was the start of a new adventure, and she was the best costar I'd ever have.

Acknowledgments

Writing this book was a *long* process. I have the attention-span of a goldfish. They say it takes a village, and it really does. Writing took time from my husband, my kids, my friends, the *laundry*—it wasn't easy. This book world also gave me some of the best friends that I will ever have. All of these people deserve a thank you for being supportive and calming my needy self.

And yeah, it's long this time, but it's my first book, so give me a little break. ;-)

First, my tripod. Y'all (see, my northern-ass can use it properly) have supported me since the first word, hashing out scenes and encouraging when I was full of self-doubt.

Kate Farlow, my person. You've been with me since I first dove into the deep-end of this world in 2016. I never thought I'd find someone eight-million miles away who shared the same soul. You are my calm, my voice of reason, my teacher, and my best friend. I freaking love you, dick. And you're getting more squeeze-hugs. #tripodforlife

Heather Orgeron, my goldfish, the only woman I'd consider polygamy with. Seriously. Where were you hiding my whole life? Thank you for loving me. Thank you for the late-night video chats, the funny kid-stories when I wanted to cry, and for always being my constant. I'd never be who I am today without you. I can't wait until we're in-laws. I love you more than shiny things. #tripodforlife

Shauna and Rachel, my real-life best friends who *totally* inspired the weird crap that comes out of Evie and Callie's mouths. You didn't even look at me like I should be institutionalized when I told you I wanted to write a book. You have supported me through every crazy dream I've ever chased, and you will always be my number ones. I love you guys.

Hilaria Alexander, what started as a trial-run has transformed into a pretty freaking amazing friendship. You've taught me so much about this industry, music, and culture. Thank you for reading some very-rough words and giving me the push I needed to finish this thing. I couldn't have done it without you, and that's the truth. I love and admire you.

Andrea Johnston, this book would NOT be the best version of itself if it weren't for you. You changed the way I thought about my characters, and challenged me to think outside the words. Your selflessness and talent and friendship are all the things I aspire to have someday. Thank you for

Dani Fusilier, Jodie Larson, Leisa Rayven, Kathy

Schofield, Kate Spitzer, Carey Heywood, Kim Jones, Becca Hensley Mysoor, Megan Addison, Marisol Scott, and so many more… this book wouldn't be what it is without you. It really *does* take a village to deal with me. Lol. I love you all SO much more than you know. You guys forever have my heart, and you'll never get rid of my needy-ass. I like you too much.

My betas/early readers/guardian angels, Dani and Kaffy– I have no words. You took a chance on me and I'm forever grateful to you.

Staci, Kandi, and Brittainy, I wouldn't even be in this world without you guys and your words. I'm so very thankful for you all. Love you all.

Alyssa Garcia, the most beautiful things come out of your brain. Thank you for dealing with my crazy and for making a cover that I'll always be in love with. You were amazing to work with and an even more amazing friend. Keep those pictures of my little diva coming!

To my editor Emily Lawrence of Lawrence Editing, this book wouldn't be anything without you. Thank you for turning something rough and jagged into the smooth, polished words I can be proud of.

To Juliana Cabrera, the format queen and an even better friend! Thank you for always making me laugh and for making my book so pretty.

To Give Me Books, THANK YOU for taking a chance on me. I don't know what I did to deserve you, but you've exceeded every expectation and more. I'm so happy to be part of the GMB family. <3

Thank you to every blogger, author, reader, and friend who has shared, read, liked a post, or supported me in any way. You are the real rockstars. Without you, my words would just be ink on a page. Thank you for taking a chance on the new kid in town.

LOLOLAND! I love you guys. I can't wait to see our weird little group grow.

To my hometown people, if you knew I was writing a book, decided to read it, and have gotten this far— thank you for still saying hi to me at the grocery store and the school when you see me in public. I love the community we live in, and I love all of you!

My parents and siblings, who are the main reason I'm this weird. Love you all, but especially a thank you to my big sister for instilling in me a love of reading and writing at such a young age. I'm so thankful you do that for so many others.

Finally, to my husband (and my babies, but they won't be reading this for about twenty years…. or *ever*.) Si, you've sacrificed the most during this rollercoaster of a book. You've stood by while I pouted, snapped, went a little *more* psycho… and you did it all with a smile and extra snuggles. Thank you for supporting my dreams, no matter what they are. You are my constant. I'm so glad I stalked you and convinced you to marry me. I love you more than anything in this world.

About The Author

Lo Brynolf was born and raised in southeast Michigan. A lover of all things artistic, Lo grew up performing on stage and in choir and attended Eastern Michigan University to major in Theater Arts. She now resides in the same small town that she grew up in with her wonderful husband and three tiny humans.

-CONNECT WITH LO-
Facebook: http://bit.ly/authorlobrynolf
Facebook (reader group): http://bit.ly/lololand
Goodreads: http://bit.ly/lobrynolfGR
Instagram: @authorlobrynolf

Made in the USA
Columbia, SC
27 March 2018